Love
Without
A Limit

M. LaShone

Sariyah

I can hear my momma's voice as Marcellus walked out the door "baby girl this is a man's world, we just living in it." She lived by those words and wanted me to as well. The tears wouldn't stop falling, no matter how many times I wiped them away. I had to pull myself together. This new client I'm meeting with in a couple of hours can make or break my career. After Marcellus slammed that door in my face mid-sentence, I realized I'm at my breaking point. That moment just kept replaying in my head as I laid in bed. I didn't sleep at all last night, fighting with myself about this man I've given my all to for the last 5 years. He has shown me he isn't trying to change.

My phone rings, though I am not in the mood to talk, I recognized the unsaved number.

"Hello, Sariyah Clinton speaking."

"Hi Sariyah, this is Jillian, wanted to confirm us meeting at 4 today at the venue?"

"Yes Jillian, I will be there at 3:45," I added with a smile.

My event planning business is my number one priority and in the past year has been doing exceptionally well. Just 6 months ago, I took a leap of faith and quit my job as a General Manager at H&M to become my own boss. Things have been great and moving forward quickly. The only thing that hasn't changed is my relationship status.

Marcellus Grant and I have been together since the beginning of time, at least that's how it feels. Like any other couple we're not perfect but who wants a perfect love story, anyway? I met him right after I graduated from college, struggling to survive on my own for the first time at 22. He's supported me through my worse struggles, which taught me to love unconditionally.

When I quit my 9-5, I made the best decision of my life. This freedom has given me more time to pursue my dreams and become more successful faster than I can ever imagine. I want the little rugrats running through the house. I want the big rock on my finger. I WANT TO BE MRS GRANT. Crazy at 27, none of these things has happened for me yet. I been making plans around pregnancies that may happen and adjusting to working all 9 months with a mini me or mini Celly inside of me. This is what I want along with success. Life is so good right now other than me wanting my man to step up and cater to all my needs since I cater to everybody else's for a living.

It has been a week since Marcellus left the house and I would be lying if I said I didn't miss him. It started off as something that could have been avoided but once we get started, there is no stopping all the shots we throw at each other. He's been staying with his aunt. She calls me every day to see if I'm ready for him to come home. Though, I don't want to fight anymore, my pride and work ethic won't let me call him. I want to focus on these upcoming events with no issues even though it's killing me to sleep alone.

"Girl I love Marcellus like a brother, but I'm starting to realize you need to leave his ass to teach him a lesson," Kaysin says as she helps herself to whatever she can find in the refrigerator.

I stare at a picture of him and I hanging up in the foyer.

"I can't just give up. I would feel like I'm throwing a major part of my life away, this isn't my home, and this isn't my life, it's our life. We share everything and feeling like he doesn't care kills me inside."

"Girl, yes you can. He doesn't realize what kind of woman he got. Maybe he does, he too stupid to show you," Kaysin laughs. "Marcellus is the one for you but at the same time, I don't want you walking around with no stupid nigga either."

Kaysin has been my best friend since our freshman year of high school. She was my partner in every class. Just because she said, "you look smart, I need a friend like you." From that day forward, she and I have been attached at the hip. Every heartbreak, accomplishment, and crazy drunk night was spent with her. She's never judged me for being with Marcellus, but she always chewed my head off when she saw me upset. She is my own personal cheerleader and therapist. I love her more than she could ever know. When I have millions, she'll have millions.

"Cellus is my everything, and he knows that. I need my space right now but his ass ain't going nowhere." I said giving Kaysin a look that reassures her I'm not leaving his ass. Marcellus is still my favorite person in the world even though I'm not fucking with him right now. He's been calling but I won't answer. I know if I answer the phone, he would be right back home quicker than I could hang up. I miss him like crazy, but he has to know what it's like to hear me say no and stand my ground.

"Girl, I can see that you already forgiving his ass in your head, but you are trying so hard to act like you don't want to answer the phone when he calls."

"Sin, you know he is going to show up eventually begging for me to take him back."
It's 4 o'clock in the afternoon and I'm just starting my day. That's the best thing about being a business owner, making your own schedule and working at a comfortable pace. I love it. I turn my laptop on and of course there he is again as my desktop picture.

"Ugh, I need to change this shit." Kaysin and I both laugh at the fact that I can't get away from him. I open my business plan with my newest client, Jillian. Last week we met at a venue where she wants to hold both her baby shower and her daughter's 5th birthday party. She is giving me a pretty penny for both events. So, these two events will be perfect. Though I am having issues in my love life that does not stop my grind. My motto is "get my money with or without any man." Marcellus knows that. I think that's one of the reasons he admires me so much. I just really wish he could show it. Honestly, it's very hard to focus because he is heavy on my mind and I want to cave in telling him "baby, just come home." I'm all over the place.
My phone rings, Kaysin looks at me and we both know exactly who is calling. Marcellus, for the hundredth time.
Before I can answer, Kaysin grabs the phone.

"Marcellus, stop calling her with your stupid ass. You keep fucking up and then want to come crawling back. My girl deserves so much better than your tired ass."

She doesn't hold her tongue but, he already knows this. She is the little sister he wishes he never met. Kaysin let him know from the jump, she was ready to fight, argue, and kill for me. Every single word she meant literally.

"Yo Sin, put Princess on the phone." Marcellus yelled.
My phone is loud enough for me to hear him say it. He gave me the name Princess when we first met. I really love when he calls me that. It makes me feel special. To this day, every time he says it, I blush. I instantly get rosy red cheeks, even with my caramel complexion. Kaysin looks at me asking with her eyes if I wanted the phone. My pride still doesn't allow me to be honest, so I play hard to get.

"Sin, tell him I said I don't feel like talking I'm busy working."

"PRINCESS, IM NOT PLAYING ANY MORE! I'm coming home tonight, and you better let me in. We are going to talk and figure this shit out." Marcellus yelled through the phone.
I can hear it in his voice, he is ready to come home. When I do let him in, he will be sleeping in the guest room and working hard to get back in the bedroom. At least that's what I want to believe.
I take the phone from Kaysin and snap back "Do what you have to do, I'm tired of all this fighting and shit. I want my man back but if you still want to be a little ass boy stay right where you are."

"That's my bitch! Yes girl, that's how you tell a nigga off. He better learn his lesson because your ass isn't leaving him," Kaysin laughs. "I'm about to get up out of here, so you can focus on your work boo. I love you and call me tonight when you finish up."

"Alright honey. I'll call you tonight." I hug her tightly and lock the door behind her.
I have to organize music and decoration patterns for the birthday party since that is coming up first. Let's get to work.

Marcellus

It seems like forever since I've been inside my apartment. This shit is crazy. I love my Princess to death, and she is getting tired of all the bullshit I'm putting her through. I'm not like these other ain't shit niggas cheating because they don't have nothing better to do. We just don't see eye to eye on a lot of things. Last time I was in the house, we had a big fight because I didn't tell her say "I love you" after she said it to me. She knows I love her, so why the hell does she need to hear it every day, when we leave each other and when we hang up the phone? As a 28-year-old man, I still don't understand women and why they overreact to everything. Saying I love you too is on top of the list from now on if that shit stops me from being in the doghouse and back at my aunt's crib.

My aunt Lisa raised me as her own when my mom decided she didn't want to be a parent anymore. She dropped me off at my aunt's house 18 years ago and never came back. For a while I was fucked up. Me and Claudia was cool, so I didn't understand why she wouldn't come back for me. She always chasing after some nigga and my pops been gone since I came into this world.

When I showed up at her house, the night Sariyah and I fought, she was sitting up in her kitchen with her glass of Patron. I never gave back my keys, and I still used them quite often.

"Celly, you scared the shit out of me. What the fuck are you doing here at 1am?" Aunt Lisa yells with a knife in hand.

"Auntie, what the hell you about to do with that?" I laugh pointing at the knife.

"About to gut you like a fish, baby boy." She looks at me up and down. "Now answer my question, you and Riyah fighting again?"

"Yes, Auntie we did. That girl is going to be the death of me."

"The death of you? Boy, that beautiful woman puts life in you. I love me some Riyah, so if you lose her, I'm gonna be the death of you."

Aunt Lisa fell in love with Sariyah the minute she laid eyes on her. After they spent hours in the kitchen talking when I brought her home for the first time, Aunt Lisa whispered in my ear "You better marry that girl." Every time my aunt talks about her, I always picture them sitting at the table together just vibing off each other's auras and it reminds me what a great woman I have. Aunt Lisa knows I am going to marry her, but if I ask her now, she would say no. Princess is over the top, she needs an extravagant proposal and not a "let me propose to you so I can make up for the bullshit I put you through." That's a sure way for her to tell me no even though deep down, her answer will always be yes.

I never been more excited about unlocking my door after this long ass week of sleeping in that uncomfortable bed at my aunt's house. When I spoke to Sariyah earlier, she told me I can come through. Actually, I demanded that she let me come back home. Either way I am here, and I hope it ain't about to be some more bullshit. To my surprise, she left the chain off the door. We had been in this 3-bedroom apartment for two years now. Sariyah picked it out after we were searching for months. We had to live with Aunt Lisa because our lease was up and didn't find an apartment that was comfortable enough to stay in long term in time. When she stepped in the door of this place for the first time, we just had to have it. At the time, it was a little over our budget, but we made it work.

To this day, she is still so in love with this apartment. The kitchen has marble counters with high stools and a full dining room attached to it. The living room is massive with huge windows. I'm not even going to get into the bedrooms. We have our master bedroom, Sariyah's office and our guest room, better known as Kaysin's room because she's always here. Everything about our place screams make yourself at home and I love that Princess made it that way.

"Princess, I'm home!" I call out hoping that she would run and embrace me like she always does.

Silence. After checking the kitchen and living room, finally I hear something

"I'm in here," she calls from her office. The sound of her voice put a smile on my face. It's dry and cold but, shit it was her voice. I don't have an apology speech, or nothing prepared, but going back to Aunt Lisa's is not an option. I want this as much as she does, now I gotta prove that shit to her.

"How you been, baby?" I approach her from behind and place a kiss on her cheek. "You been missing a nigga, that's a fact."

"Marcellus, don't come up in here with that bullshit like I'm supposed to be ecstatic that you are here. What do you want, honestly? I'm not about to sit and listen to the same sorry ass shit you been telling me. I've had enough of that and I'm done."

Damn, why the fuck is she being this cold to me? Normally after a fight, I give her space and by the time I come home she is ready with open arms She is serious this time, shit wasn't even that serious. "Yo, you really mad because I didn't say I love you back?"

If looks could kill, I would be dead ten times over. Princess looks so hurt and let down. She has never been like this toward me. Shit has me fucked up.

"It's not about you not saying, 'I love you too'. It's about you knowing and understanding me. We been doing this shit for 5 years now. Like how the fuck you don't know what makes me happy? or is it that you do know what makes me happy, you just choose not to do that shit? Is it that fucking hard to love me and show me that you are 100 percent in this? I am showing you that I can't see myself with anybody but you. I could've left a long time ago, but I didn't. I'm still here and clearly, I'm not going any fucking where whether I want to or not."

At this point, she's in full blown tears. As a man, I don't have many weaknesses but one, for sure, is seeing Princess cry. Sariyah is one of the two strongest women I know. So, when she starts crying, that shit does something to me. At this point things have to change or I'm going to lose her for good.

"I'm tired and you know exactly what you need to do. The ball is in your court for the last time. I really hope you don't foul out." Sariyah spoke those words like they were her final. I don't understand what I'm missing. I didn't think she was this upset about the `dispute we had. We have had major fights in the past. I'm not the perfect man, but I am good to her. She may think that I am not ready for anything more but I am. I don't know how to show her. I made it seem like I was doing the best I could but deep down the type of nigga she wants, I gotta work hard to be. Not as a man but as her companion. Females always talking this "I need a real man, a companion, their equal." Shit I didn't know anything about that, but I guess I was about to find out.

"Princess, I love you and I'm not gonna sit here and explain how and why because you already see that. We been doing this for 5 years now.

I didn't even get the full sentence out, she cut me off, "Marcellus, what is this? I'm your girlfriend. Been the same for some time. No moving forward and no growth. Nothing has changed between us. Seems like it's been the same routine for the past 3 years. I am not about to settle because you can't figure out what the fuck you want." She knows I hate when she uses our relationship and settle in the same sentence. It got to me so bad, I lost it.

"Settle? so now being with me you're settling? You act like you did this shit by yourself. I have been your number one fucking supporter when you didn't have shit, but your stupid ass always forgets that when you try to prove a point. This shit here is ours, both of our names are on this lease. Sariyah, this is our fucking relationship. You and me. We built this together and we are going to build a family and a house, and all that fairy tale shit you want. But, if you settling, you probably should walk now."

This is always how our arguments start and end. Damn, now I see why she says it's the same routine because this is what we do on a regular. My first instinct is to apologize, but that's what I always do. So, I already know what her reaction is going to be. I stared at her waiting for a response.

"Marcellus, if I could, I would have. But I guess that's how this shit goes between us. It's fucked up and we need to figure what we want for real. I'm not about to waste more time trying to show you how to love me or make me happy."

Sariyah turns and walks out the office. Before I could reply, she made her way to our master bedroom. A few minutes later, I got a text from her saying "Guest Room or Couch but you not about to sleep next to me until you deserve to." I don't even feel like arguing anymore. I head to our guest room, happy to be in the comfort of my home even though Princess isn't fucking with me. Let's see how long this is gonna last.

Sariyah

Knowing Marcellus is in the guest room and not lying next to me is killing me inside. I can't put my pride aside after the things he said. He has to sleep in there for at least one night. His presence in the house put me at ease but I'm still very confused about what I want to do. If I walk now, that's the ultimate defeat in my eye and I didn't want to experience that, especially not with the love of my life. This isn't us. I'm supposed to have his last name and bare his first child. I did this every time we had an argument and still, I am here being the best girlfriend I can be. That is the number one issue. I'm tired of being a girlfriend because I deserve to be his wife. He has a lot of issues he needs to work out within himself. My heart will not allow me to leave. He deserves to be loved like he has never been loved before. Since the day I found out everything he had been through. I vowed to be that person and more. I didn't realize it would be this hard or this draining.

Not knowing where we will end up scares me the most. I hope he starts to make the right decisions before I walk away and not give a second thought to turn back. As my eyes get heavy, I tie up my hair and convince myself not to call him in the room to cuddle.

I wake up to the aroma of eggs and bacon. I can't help but smile. Marcellus is in the kitchen cooking. That's one thing I can count on when he is home, there will be a nice home cooked meal. I can't even boil macaroni. Anything I couldn't handle, he was always there to pick up the pieces.

It instantly takes me back to our first date where Marcellus had to battle the biggest burden in my life, my mother. He did nothing but, shower me with compliments and made me smile. On that day was the clarification that I wanted to spend my life with him.

July 7, 2012

I am pacing back and forth in my room in agony. Marcellus just texted me and told me he is on his way. I'm not ready for a date. My hair is a mess, and I just got off work. Before I could tell him no, he hung up on me.

"Ma, what should I do? I really like him." Although I am elated that he has been persistent about taking me out on a date for weeks now, it can't be today. It isn't the right time.

"Riy, tell his ass to go home when he gets here. You look a hot ass mess, tryna go on a date," Santina said.

Why did I even say anything to her? She is always so fucking negative. She swears she is a licensed relationship guru, but her ass is still single.

"Mom, I'm not gonna send him home and miss my chance with my future husband and baby daddy, I'm going on this date." I wash up quickly, put on a tube top and high-waisted shorts with some heels. After looking in the mirror, I can see that I am showing a lot so, I cover up with a long-knit cardigan I got from H&M. I love my natural hair, but my mother hates it. No matter what style it is in she always says the same shit. This time though, it was so true. Natural hair isn't a two-minute style type of hair. I put it into a high bun and lay down my edges. For, fifteen minutes I'm looking like a bad little joint. As soon as I'm about to take a second glance in the mirror, he calls.

"Hey Celly, are you here already?"

"Yes, Princess. I'm about to ring the bell."

"No, don't." But before I can finish my sentence, I hear the bell ring and he is off my line.

I do not want him to meet my mother yet. She is someone you had to meet in doses.

"Sariyah, your future husband and baby daddy is here. That's what you called him earlier right?" Santina let out a laugh that made the whole floor shake.

Not only am I embarrassed, I'm also angry with her. She loves making a fool out of me every chance she gets. I don't want to come out of my room, but I can't leave him out there or she might start telling stories and pulling out pictures of when I was in my awkward, ugly stage.

"Hey." I smile at Marcellus, but he knows I am one hundred percent embarrassed.

"Princess, you clean up nice."

"Who the fuck is Princess?" My mother just won't let up. "Last time I checked I named her Sariyah Jhene Clinton."

"No disrespect, Ms. Clinton. I am sure that your daughter is a princess, so ever since the day I met her, that has been what I've called her."

"Oh god, so you are one of those smooth talkers. That ain't no princess, she is looking like a peasant with that damn natural hair so untamed."

In my mind, I am calling my mother all types of bitches and hoes. But I am never disrespectful to her. Even though the way she raised me, she always told me not to be scared and speak my mind. Honestly, she doesn't want to know what I really think about her.

"Her natural hair is beautiful, I love when she has a twist out. I hit her up on short notice so that's why she decided on the bun. That's my second favorite, so I can see her beautiful face." Marcellus isn't letting my mother dog me out in front of him.

"Damn you good boy, hope you have condoms cuz you can surely talk a woman out of her panties."

"Alright, alright ma, that's enough. Let's Go Celly." Before she can respond, I push Marcellus out the door.

"What the hell was that?" He questions me as soon as we were on the other side.

"That right there, was my mother Santina Clinton, a handful, isn't she?"

"Princess, that's an understatement." Marcellus says as he opens my car door. He mumbles something, but I don't catch it.

As soon as he gets in, I'm ready to fight, "What you said about my mother?"

"Nothing shorty, what I said was I wonder what my mother is like, but that's for another day."

Sadness showed all over his face, but I didn't push the subject. We will get to it when the time is right.

Thinking about that day I realize once again why I fell in love with him. Though my pride still has me in my feelings, I am ready to give in to him. I go to the bathroom and shower because as soon as I step out into that kitchen, it'll be time to make up. I throw on my Pink sports bra and leggings.

As I walk to the kitchen, he greets me with a kiss and my plate already made.

"I was just about to wake your ass up, you sleep so late." Marcellus said with confidence. We are both over the argument.

"I been up, took a shower and all, even brushed my teeth," I wave my hand in front of my face, "which apparently you didn't because your breath is kicking." It's time for us to get on the same page.

I sit down at our high countertop and eat. Marcellus just stares at me, which he does often after we have fights.

"Why are you staring at me? That shit is so creepy." I couldn't help but start laughing which makes him laugh.

"Princess, I apologize about last night and last week. Shit, I'm just sorry. I love you girl and right now shit isn't that sweet between us. But shorty I have plans, big plans."

"Okay, babe." I didn't say much because I heard this speech before and I'm not about to be telling him everything was all forgiven when deep down I still have my doubts.

"Princess, can I ask you a question?" Marcellus approaches me and run his fingers through my hair.

"That is a question, Celly, what do you want?" I giggle because the bedroom is exactly where we are headed.

"Why the fuck you look so good, it has been a week, and a nigga is on swole so please let me take you to the room and show you how much I miss you."

Who was I not to obliged?

As he carries me to our bedroom, this is about to be the best make up sex we ever had. He throws me on the bed and rips my clothes off. I was in shock because he was never this aggressive and to be honest; I am really enjoying this.

"You was missing this dick?" His massive dick growing in his briefs controls my body and instantly I was flowing like Niagara Falls.

"Yes, baby." I get out between my moans. Marcellus kisses me from head to toe and when he got to my clit and pussy, I almost lost my mind. He is tearing me up like we didn't just have breakfast and he is starving. I can't contain my screams and can't wait to put his dick in my mouth and suck the soul out of his body. Every time I try to move, he sticks his tongue deeper inside of me.

"I'm sorry baby, I love you so much." Him breathing on me was such a turn on and it was time for me to take control.

"Celly, pull your dick out." I grab his head and stare him straight in the eyes. Without hesitation, he stops and pulls it out. My eyes grow so big. After all this time, I still get overly excited when his veins start popping out of his dick when he is hard. I suck and gag on it and he loves every minute.

"Oh shit, right there, Princess. DON'T STOP." His moans make me go even harder and faster. "Shit slow down, I need to feel that pussy."

I stop sucking and bend over in front of him with my hands grabbing the edge of our bed. He enters me, and I swear it was like the first time all over again.

"Yea, baby, you feel how tight this pussy is for you?"

"Princess, I feel that shit, it's warm and tight."

"Juicy." I start cumming all over him.

"SHIT! I'm about to cum." He creams inside of me and collapses on top of my body. He kisses all over my neck. "Damn, I missed my pussy."

It seems like we have been fucking all day. Though the sex is beyond amazing and I was really missing his dick, I'm still torn about giving it up so easily and not making him wait. I am such a sucker when it comes to him. I know exactly what I want and though he talks a good game, I am ready for actions. He looks so handsome lying there asleep or, so I thought. He startles me when he speaks.

"Princess, we gonna get this right. I'm sorry for all the shit I put you through and how inconsistent I can be. I just have my insecurities about being able to give you the kind of love you deserve. I want to give you the world, but that shit is hard. I love you more than I ever thought I could love any female. You bring out the best in me and the worse in me. I really want to make you happy, but I been so fucked when it comes to giving my all."

It brings tears to my eyes. He never tells me what he is feeling. Everything that he has been through with his mother has him afraid to give me his all, but I'm willing to show him it is possible to love and not be left.

"Cellus, you have never said no shit like that to me before and honestly it's showing that you want whatever it is that I want. We both have a lot of shit to work on. I can be selfish sometimes, but mostly because I'm selfless all the time. We will get to where we need to be, I promise. I know from experience, these years have not been a walk in the park but I'm still here, right?"

"Princess, just bear with me a little while longer, baby. I promise you I just want to be sure I'm capable because you been ready."

All the doubt and insecurities I have are slowly fading away. Marcellus doesn't have faith in himself, so I have enough for the both of us. I am going to wait however long he needs me to. I can't see myself with anyone else. Call me crazy, but for him, that's exactly what I am.

Kaysin

I decide to call Sariyah since the last time I spoke to her was 2 days ago after I left her house.

Normally, she would call me after she finished up all of her work. She is all that I have left, and she is the best thing that's ever happen to me. Saving my life on countless occasions and always being there for me made her top priority in my life. I'm far from perfect but, she has never left my side despite all the bad decisions I've made. A friendship like ours is hard to find these days.

"Riyah, why the hell you didn't call me yesterday?"

"My bad girl, Cellus came home and we good now." I let out a sigh of relief when she said Marcellus was home. My girl loves her man and I know he is perfect for her. He is just a man that does man shit. "What happened sis?"

"I met somebody and girl when I tell you he is fine. Brown skin, handsome and body looking good." I'm beaming talking about him. "Girl he is just my type."

"I say the same shit to you, niggas always doing some fuck shit to you. So, take it slow, and I mean snail slow. I mean grandma with a cane slow. Bitch, wait 2 weeks to text him slow." She always gives me this speech when it comes to me meeting guys. We can all agree, my choice in men is not the best and I'm always getting hurt or end up in some crazy situation. This time I really hope it is different. I'm gonna listen to her and wait before pursuing anything with a new person. I have skeletons I need to get rid of before I give my all to someone new.

"Alright girl, we can do brunch tomorrow, so get reacquainted with your man. I love you."

"I love you too Sin."

There is a knock at my door, and I am not excepting company. So, I automatically put my guard up.

"Who is it?" No response, I start to head towards my bedroom, I don't want to be bothered.

They knock again, this time with more power.

"Who the fuck is it? I'm not about to open the door to no stranger, so either say something or stay outside."

"Sin, baby open the door." That is a voice I do not miss at all and the only way he is going to leave is if I let him in.

"Jay, what do you want?" I say as I open the door. "I don't have time to play no games with you. Go home to your little girlfriend."

"I miss you, that bitch ain't doing nothing but nagging me about how much I should be over here with you." I laugh right in his face. He knows he has me fucked up.

Jay was the love of my life and I worshipped the ground he walked on. That was until he started cheating with little miss Asia. Asia was one of those girls you want to drag every time you see her. She wants to make my life a living hell like I was the one who did wrong.

"Jay, shut the hell up and get out. You don't miss me, you think that you can have your cake and eat it too." I begin getting irritated with repeating myself. "Baby, I am nobody seconds and damn sure ain't about to be dealing with Asia crazy ass. She don't want to see that side of me Jay. So, go home."

"I am home, Kaysin." Jay says with desperation in his eyes.

"Jay, let's not start this. This hasn't been your home for months and I worked hard to get rid of every memory of you in this place. Now this is my home and you being here right now is messing up the energy in here.

"Sin, are you seriously telling me that you don't miss me and all the memories we made in this house and with each other?"

"Yes, that's exactly what I am saying. You made your bed so now you can lay in it without me. Forget about me and every memory we share."

After finding about Jay and Asia, I decided to walk away from the toxic relationship him and I shared. That wasn't the first time he cheated on me. For the first two years, our relationship was beautiful, and he was everything I thought I wanted. Soon after I told him, I wanted to get married and make babies, things quickly changed. He started getting calls in the middle of the night and staying out all night. I acted oblivious to the obvious. I was far from stupid but was blinded with what I thought was love. It wasn't until I walked in on him and Asia in our bed. I completely lost my mind and nearly killed them both. Jay was convinced I was going to take him back because I stayed all the other times he cheated. Walking in on the man you are ready to spend your life with another woman is the deal breaker. I really dodged a bullet because now he is with Asia doing the same shit to her that he was doing to me. I am so good on that chapter in my life.

"Sin, stop playing games with me and let me come home. I was just fucking with them girls I was gonna get right back."
It really irks me when he tries to make a joke to lighten the mood that shit is not funny. Him being in my presence and having to relive all the hurt and pain I went through during our breakup infuriates me and makes me want to slap the skin off his face. He is staring at me to see if any emotions show on my face and I can honestly say there isn't because I don't have any. When you give your all to someone and they blatantly disrespect you and your feelings, you learn to be emotionless.

"Baby girl, I am sorry. I realize that I don't want to be with Asia. She was there, and shit just happened. It was a mistake and I'm still regretting the day I met her. I miss you and this." He steps forward and tries to grab my arm. I pull away and at this point it is time for him to go.

"This is the last fucking time I am going to say this to you so please listen to me carefully. Jayceon, you will never ever get me back in your life, not as your girlfriend nor your friend. I don't even want to be your enemy. I don't hate you even though I really want to. I just want you to leave me the fuck alone, so I can move on with my life. And give all this good loving to someone who deserves it, not your lying cheating ass."
Jay looks at me like I'm Medusa and proceeds towards to the door. Normally he says something smart but to my surprise, he shocks me again.

"Damn Sin, I really fucked up with you. You don't deserve the shit I put you through. You a goddess baby girl. And I promise you, this nigga is going to change and I'm gonna get you back shorty."

"Please don't waste your time, my mind has been made up since that day." This nigga is trippin' always tryna to touch me, he reaches for me one too many times. My blood begins to boil and me being cordial is out of the question

"Jayceon, get the fuck out of my house now. You are so full of shit and excuses. God blessed me the day he showed your true colors. I really dodged a bullet. You and Asia are made for each other because both of you are delusional."

I look at him with no remorse and push him towards the door.

"Don't come back here again. Good fucking riddance."

As soon as I lock my door, the tears start falling down my face. I'm a good person who always ends up being hurt. I am tired of being the one hurt and sad. I need to find happiness within myself and let the chips fall where they may.

After crying myself to sleep, I wake up with puffy eyes and wild hair. I am always so hard on myself and wonder why I am put in situations I can't handle. Jay will somehow make his way back to my apartment but next time, he won't get any of my time. I should get a restraining order on his ass, but it really isn't that deep. I get up and head to my bathroom. I need a hot shower and some Trey Songz radio on Pandora. My Bluetooth speaker mounted on my wall, blasted "Slow Motion." I am so passionate about music. I love to sing and dance, but I would never pursue a career from it. It's the calm after the storm for me. I am a perfectionist. I am never fully satisfied with the outcome of things unless it is done completely right. Looking in the mirror before getting in the shower, I can't help but admire my beauty. I have confidence on the outside. I am what niggas these days call slim thick. My caramel complexion matches my curly brown hair. I'm not out here looking like these Instagram models, but I give myself a solid 8. I hop in the shower and sing along with every song that plays. Even after all the tears I have shed, I am overcoming another heartbreak with faith and prayer on my mind hoping I will never have to experience that pain again.

Once again, I catch a glimpse in the mirror when my phone rings. I don't recognize the number, so I am hesitating to answer knowing it is probably Jay's psychotic ass.

"Hello," The tone of my voice clearly gave away the fact I was clueless.

"Oh, so you didn't save my number. Damn shorty." The voice is still unfamiliar. My first instinct to hang up and block the number but once again, my curious ass continues the conversation.

"I apologize, but who this is and was I supposed to save your number?"

"Kaysin, it's that handsome brown skinned bearded man you saw the other night on your way home." His reference makes me laugh, why would I say that to him, minutes after meeting him?

I am relieved he called first because as I promised Sariyah I would not call him for about 3 weeks.

"My bad, Adonis. I was gonna save it, just didn't get around to it yet. Your number was already in my phone from when you called me that night, but just nameless." I chuckle knowing he may be in his feelings about my statement.

"I guess I'll let you slide because your little cute ass is coming to dinner with me tonight."

"No, I am not, and that's not how you ask a woman on a date."

"One thing you will learn about me is I rarely ask questions and I always get what I want. And tonight, I want to go to dinner with you. So, meet me at Ricardo's at 9 o'clock. I know you need time to get yourself together so I'm giving you that. Don't stand me up."
His demeanor and tone are already turning me on, and lord knows I love a man who takes charge.

"Okay this is not a date, just two acquaintances sharing a meal, you pay for your meal and I'll pay for mine."

"Yea okay, I will see you at 9 and don't be late. I already made reservations. Later beautiful,"

"See you later Adonis."
After hanging up the phone, I am smiling way too hard and I am about to use the next 4 hours to get myself glammed. My ass is gonna be a 10 tonight. I straighten my hair. My curls are cute but when my hair is straightened, I feel so sexy and it also adds a few inches to my length. Whenever I need to channel my alter ego, I play Beyoncé. That bitch always has me feeling like a million bucks. After about 2 hours, I'm still in my closet looking for the perfect outfit. I haven't entertained the idea of talking to another man since Jay left about 4 months ago. I don't

know what it was about Adonis that made me stop and give him my number, but I need two things I have been missing, dick and affection. Not like I plan on giving it up on the first night but just the thought of a man makes me tingle all over. Finally, I decide on a red strapless dress with my Christian Louboutin's heels. I have to say that I look completely different from the person he met the other night, and I am happy about that. I contemplate on if I should tell Sariyah that I agreed to go on the date with him, but I'll just wait until our brunch tomorrow. I put on some light makeup and a bomb red lip. Just as I finish applying my lipstick, my phone buzzes.

Adonis: One hour, baby girl. Can't wait to see you!
Me: I'm about to head out now.

I say a little prayer before walking out the door. Lord please let this man be nothing like any of these crazy men I have encountered in my lifetime. I am ready to settle down and have some babies. So, lord help a sister out! Amen.

Adonis

I pull up to the restaurant a few minutes early, so I can be front row when Kaysin pulls up. I need to admire her beauty for a minute. When we ran into each other a few nights ago, she got me all out of character. I ain't the nigga to chase a female and I damn sure don't ask them for their number. Kaysin caught my attention, and I would have felt like an idiot if I had let her walk away. Tonight, she looks so different and shorty is beautiful. I caught her slipping, and she was still bad as fuck. This dress she has on has me adjusting my pants. This is just a little dinner date and she looking like a model about to walk down a red carpet runway. Great minds think alike, we both wearing red which is my favorite color. Fuck! I'm underdressed, my simple GStar Raw t-shirt and GStar jeans with my red and white 11s, makes me want to go home and change. Kaysin got me pleased already, and tonight is gonna be hard.

Commitment ain't in my vocabulary. Kaysin is definitely the committed type but, I couldn't help myself. I am a man and I have a healthy appetite for women. My biggest problem is leading woman on and somehow, they claim we are something we aren't. It ain't even my fault they fall so hard. These females always want to jump right into relationships. You should date first, learn about the nigga and a relationship may or may not be on the list. Everybody don't need a title. If you on your shit, you don't need to worry about anything. Now Kaysin looks like she is on her shit, not needing a man to define who she is as a woman. That's the type of shit I like.

Kaysin: I'm here and it's 8:55. You better be here by 9 or I am leaving

Me: Calm down tiger, I just parked my whip. Be there in a second.

This girl is going to give me a run for my money and I will enjoy every moment. I step out of my 2017 Audi A6, I feel like I'm about to meet Michelle Obama. She is always gonna be the first lady in my eyes. My nerves are all over the place but with my confidence and swag, you can't tell. As I walk across the street, Kaysin makes eye contact with me and I rethink my life values. This woman is giving me all type of feelings without saying a word.

"Damn shorty, where we going after this?"

"Oh stop, It's a simple dress and heels,"

"And straight hair which I like. You did not look like this the other night. Not saying you wasn't looking good but damn the switch up is real. Oh, shit is that a wig or weave." I am serious about my compliments to her and I didn't want to seem thirsty, so I threw that joke in, her real hair is clear as day. For the rest of the night, I will be forward but not as much as I want to say, "let's skip dinner and head back to my place."

"Thank you, you not looking too bad yourself and this is my real hair asshole." She winks and walks in front of me toward the door and I can't help but stare at her ass. It isn't huge, but it ain't little either. For a slim joint, Kaysin is nice in all the right places and I am enjoying my view.

"Do you have a reservation?" The hostess says making direct contact. That shit makes me more nervous.

"Yes, should be under the name Adonis Carter for 9pm." I am trying not to look at Kaysin too hard but, damn she is beautiful. She is standing there with so much poise and I am not used to a female not being all in my shit. She ain't checking for me too hard and she didn't stare at the hostess with the "this is my man, so back off bitch" face.

"Okay Mr. Carter, your table will be ready in just a minute, please step to the side and I will call your name soon."

I grab Kaysin's hand and lead her to the waiting area.

"Thank you for accepting my offer to spend your Saturday night with me."

"Remember, this is just two friends grabbing a bite to eat."

"Oh, so you wearing red bottoms to friends grabbing a bite to eat."

Kaysin laughs while running her fingers through her hair. She already called me an asshole. I am tryna say all the right things, but I like to be honest. By the end of the night, only one thing will be on my mind.

"Mr. Carter, your table is ready." Kaysin takes the lead and lets me follow behind her. I guess I haven't been out with a lady in a while because I am a kid in a candy store with the way she is carrying herself. As soon as we sit down, she doesn't waste any time to pry information out of me.

"So, Adonis Carter, what's your story?"

"Damn, a nigga can't even order the food yet?" I'm fucking with her and seems like she is ready to play any game I want to play.

"Nope, because I'm not about to get comfortable and have to get up in the middle of my meal because you say something I don't like. So, before we get our food, will this meal be to go or to stay?" Our waiter comes over, "Hello, my name is Andrea. I'll be your server tonight. Can I start you with something to drink?"

"White or Red?" I ask Kaysin as she pretends to be scanning the menu.

"Whatever you like, I don't mind either one."

"Okay, can I get a bottle of white wine, please? You can choose, you know these shits better than us."

"No problem, coming right up, are you ready to order food also?"

"I am, Filet Mignon. Medium well but little to no pink, please." Kaysin knows exactly what she wants which means she has been here before.

"I'll take the Surf N Turf."
We close our menus and hand them to the waiter.

"Now back to you." She has a mission to complete.

"Aight, what you want to know?"

"I want to know you, anything and a little bit of everything."

"Adonis is my name. I am the CEO of my barber shop located in the Bronx. My pops handed it down to me and it been making bank so now I'm chillin' and reaping the benefits. I am 28 and my birthday is November 15th."

"This is not a dating site." She mocks me which is hilarious. "Let's cut the bullshit we are grown."

"But wait, let me give you my dating site bio too. Kaysin is my name. I am not a CEO, but I am the HR Director for a huge retail company. Hiring and firing everyone for all the stores. I make enough money to wear these red bottoms. I am 27 and my birthday is February 9th.

"Okay, Ms. Director. I see you. Maybe we can go into business together. I boss you around and you boss them around."

Our bottle of champagne arrives, and this liquid courage will tell her things I don't want her to find out.

"You can never boss me around, baby I can upgrade you."

"So, Kaysin, why you here with me and not at home cuddling up with a man?"

"Niggas ain't shit and can't appreciate a good woman even if one slap them in the face."

"Whoa, you went from 0 to 100 real quick, what is that about?"

"Since we keeping it real, I'm gonna put you on now I'm not with the games. I'm gonna always tell you what you don't want to hear and mean it. I'll bring this up once and never speak on it again."

She chugs the wine that's in her glass which makes me nervous.

"My ex cheated on me with someone nowhere near my caliber. Till this day, he keeps coming to my door saying she was a mistake, and he is ready to come home. He will never be in my home again. And if you are a cheater, you will never get in my home period. I'm not playing that shit."

"Alright, that's fair. I will say this. I am single, but there are a few women checking for me. Not to say I'm checking for them, but I entertain them and talk to them."

"Check please," She says laughing.

"This is going well, and honesty is hard to come by anymore so I 'preciate yours." I wasn't about to let her walk out that door. "I'm sure we will run into this nigga so at least I have the heads up."

"You are being honest about your groupie entourage which I didn't expect coming from a handsome gentleman like yourself. So, I guess I can stay, and we can be friends," She smirks with her sarcastic ass.

Shorty has me ready to sit here all night and listen to her talk, but this ain't gonna last forever.

Jayceon

Watching Kaysin laugh and flirt with this nigga has me pissed the fuck off. I can't believe that she is really on a date or whatever the fuck this is. I followed Kaysin here after she left her house today. This girl has me on my stalker shit. I been following her for the last month. When I first realized she wasn't trying to let me back in the house, I couldn't believe that shit. I needed to see why or who was stopping me from going back home to the love of my life. Asia was really supposed to be a little fling but once Kaysin kicked me out, I started chilling with her more and we ended up living together. Asia is a beautiful dark-skinned joint with the best natural body I've ever seen in my life, but her insecurities and bad attitude makes her so ugly sometimes. It's been about 4 months and I've been over Asia since the second one. She will never amount to the woman Kaysin is, and I made a stupid ass decision. Now I am living with it.

I recognize the nigga from the other night when they had their little exchange. I was going to mention it to Kaysin when I ran up to her house earlier today but then she would know that I've been watching her and start being more cautious of her surroundings. She was already super cautious, carrying pepper spray and a pocketknife in her purse. I don't want her to stab my ass up thinking I'm some crazy nigga tryna rob her or something. Everything about Kaysin makes a nigga happy but I never want to settle down and be a family man. That shit scares me and the fact that Kaysin wants it so bad makes me want to run away from her. I am selfish and can't see myself without her even though I don't want any of the shit she wants. So, I keep women on the side just to reassure myself that I'm not about to be tied down to any female. I was lying to Kaysin telling her I changed and wanted to be a better man for her. I just want to get back in her house because she treats me like royalty, and I love it. But, seeing her on a date with another man is making my veins pop out my skin and ready to kill this nigga.

My phone starts going off and it's Asia with her annoying ass. I can't breathe too hard without her accusing me of cheating on her.

"Jayceon, where are you? You been gone all day and haven't called me once." Asia whines into the phone.

"Asia, I left a couple hours ago, and we live together. Why do I have to call you when I step out the door?" I shouldn't have answered the phone when I saw her name pop up but to avoid her bitchin' and her starting another argument, I answer.

"Did you go to that bitch's house today? What does she have that I don't?"

"Cut the shit Asia, stop comparing the two of you. You and her are two different people."

"And for some reason, you keep running back to her ass like she is God's gift to the earth."

"So, you call me to argue, I don't have time for this shit and I don't want to deal with this shit when I get home."

"Jay, just hurry up and come home. So, I can stop thinking you are out there doing shit."

I hang up the phone and sit back in my car wondering how the hell I had Kaysin and ended up with Asia.

"Damn, where the fuck they went?" I look up and Kaysin is gone.

I almost want to pull up to her crib but I'm not in the mood to cause a scene and possibly murk somebody tonight. Before I go home to deal with drama, Imma slide to another shorty's crib to ease my mind, so I can be ready for the bullshit.

When I get to shorty's crib, she ain't opening the fucking door to let me in.

"Yo, what the fuck is your problem?" I start banging on the door. "I'm not in the mood for your shit."

"Jayceon, I don't need to be anybody's side piece. Ya bitch called me and told me all about your living situation and how you in a whole relationship."

"What the fuck you talking about." Asia got me fucked up, going through my phone. "Let me in, I can show you, you the only girl I need."

"Fuck you, Jay."

"Fuck you too, bitch. Don't call me when you want some of this."

"Don't hold your breath, dummy."

Now I'm going home to this stupid nagging bitch, I already want to slam her for going through my phone. I gotta get my Kaysin back, this bitch gonna make me kill her.

These last few days have been amazing and the reality I been longing for. Marcellus has been catering to my every need like he has never done before. I don't know what it was about this last argument we had but I feel like I am with a different person. He has been hinting at a proposal and trying to give me a baby every chance he gets. He helped me organize my planner for the rest of the month and is listening to all the ideas for my upcoming events and giving me feedback. I'm the happiest I've been in a while and I hope this bliss stays the same.

"Cellus, what time are you going to Aunt Lisa's?" I say while applying my makeup to meet Kaysin for brunch. Though these last few days been beautiful, I miss my best friend and I know she is in need one of our therapy sessions.

"You can meet me there at 6. I know when you and Sin get together, the time is non-existent, and Auntie said bring her with you. She is missing her girls."
Aunt Lisa and I share a great relationship even when Marcellus and I are bad terms. She is the mother I wish I had though my mother is still alive and well. My mother believes my success is her success and only calls me when she is in need. For years, my mother has disliked Lisa and our bond. I appreciate it and will give her my last. Kaysin and I are the daughters she illegally adopted, and she loves us unconditionally.

"Kaysin will be so excited. She has nobody so when it's family time, she lights up like a Christmas tree."

"I know babe and though she gets on my damn nerves, I love her like a sister. So, tell her crazy ass to bring liquor too so we can turn up."

"Celly, I gotta focus on Jillian's events this week. Y'all not about to get me drunk as a skunk and unable to get up for these meetings tomorrow."

My phone rings "That's my main one, That's my main one." My Main by Mila J is me and Kaysin's anthem and she insisted that it be our ringtones for each other. Her and Marcellus are the only ones with ringtones I paid for. Everyone else has that generic ass iPhone ringtone.

Hey baby love, are you ready?"

"Yes, Riy Riy, I have so much to tell you and I can't wait to see you.

"I know girl, I'm about to walk out the door. I'll come pick you up, I wasn't going to drive but remember it's Sunday, so parking regulations don't matter today."

"Umm, nah we are splitting an Uber downtown, your drunk ass will not be driving me anywhere."

"Girl you right, oh yea let's call this a pre-game because it's Sunday dinner at Aunt Lisa's.

"Yasssss, this weekend has been just what I needed." Kaysin says with too much energy. So, I know something happened with her, I need to hurry and get to her.

"Alright bitch, I'm on my way. You know my bougie ass is taking an Uber to you."

"Riyah, it's like a 10 min walk from your crib to mine."

"And with these 6-inch heels it will feel like 20, so Uber it is." Kaysin already knows how I roll. I will take an Uber or drive to the corner store if I didn't get backlash from Marcellus.

We say our goodbyes and I finish up my hair which is pinned up in 2 buns and let my bangs fall right below my eyes. There was a certain glow as I look in the mirror.

"Thanks Marcellus." I say smiling.

"For what?" Marcellus approaches me from behind and grabs my waist.

"For showing me, you can be the man I know you can be. Now let me go before I don't make it to Kaysin."

"I'll call her back if you want me too."

"No, thank you nasty, I'll see you later." We laugh, and he walks me to the door.

"You look like a meal, fuck a snack."

"Thanks baby, I'll see you at 6 and I hope I'm not already drunk." I pull my phone out to call for my Uber.

Though the Uber ride is short, it was the only time I have to myself. I send a follow up email to my client to brush up the details for next weekend's event and make sure she knows of all the meetings and that the invoices are up to date.

My life is coming together, and I'm just hoping nothing is going to fuck it up and knock me off my high horse.

Kaysin

"Girl, I don't know how I ended up at his place, we finished that bottle before we even got our food."
Sariyah may not agree with the way things went down last night but she never judges me.

"Sin, you slept with him?" Sariyah was on her fourth mimosa just taking in all the other non - alcoholic tea I'm giving her.

"No, girl. I'm not that type of girl." She gives me a look like 'bitch please'. "No for real, I've changed my life. I wasn't ready to go home, and he offered that we go back to his place and chill. At first, I was against it, but you know I ALWAYS keep my pepper spray and knife so if he got out of line, I was definitely going to protect myself."

"I can't even be mad at you girl because you actually listened to me, but you had the nigga so open, he hit you up the next day."

"Ya girl still got it." We clicked glasses. "When we got to his place, he was a perfect gentleman and Riyah this man is paid. Like his penthouse was beautiful, I'm pretty sure his mother decorated his apartment because everything was color coordinated and well put together. It had a woman's touch."

"Bitch, you better clarify that next time you see him because he might have a whole wife who is out of town on business."
Sariyah is referring to my "Adam" situation. A few years back, I thought I found the man of my dreams until I found out he was married with four children. His wife was a flight attendant who traveled a lot. His kids generally stayed with his mother because they both had crazy

work schedules. I found out he was married when his wife called me to tell me she found the pictures of us boo'ed up at our weekend getaway to Atlantic City. So, I let him be with his wife and never looked back. We both get a kick out of that time in my life and still to this day can't believe how that whole thing played out.

"Nah, he is single and gladly plays the field entertaining many females. He was very honest with me, so I'm definitely going to get more information before I let him get a taste of Sin."

"Ain't that the truth." Sariyah sighs. "Sin, I love Marcellus."

"Umm, yea I know that Riy." Now her ass is drunk and she about to start the "I love Marcellus" speech.
She starts to laugh which turns into tears, "I just really want us to get it right, Sin. I love him so much and when I'm around him, I feel like a beautiful soul, a completed soul"

"Baby love, you are a beautiful soul with or without Marcellus. You are my beautiful soul. For years, you have held me down and no matter what shit I bring to you, you will always have my back. Marcellus loves you and we both know that my god children will be coming into this world sooner than later. Ya'll asses give me hope and every time ya'll fight I'm like lord please get my sister back to her man because I can't take seeing you with your heart broken."

"Thanks Sin Sin, I really need that. Fuck friends, we are sisters. I love you more than the woman that birthed me."

"Whoa what happened now? Riyah, when is the last time you spoke to her?"

"It's been at least a month, I guess that $2500 last time I saw her is enough for her for the month. But rent is about to be due so I'm sure she will be calling my phone soon asking for some money."

"Your mother loves you. She just has a funny way of showing it."

"She feels like I owe her because she gave me life and I just don't think that is fair. My childhood was wonderful but when I became a teenager, she treated me more like a friend and that's when I needed her the most."

"Riyah, I know you wish things were different and she would be here for you more but, let me tell you something, I never had a mother or father and I just wish I had either one to give money too. It's a whole different feeling when she isn't there at all. All I've had is you and Mama Jean. When she passed, I felt like I had to go with her. You were there to love me like no one ever did and I am forever grateful for that. You have a heart of gold despite whatever revelations your mother gives you always remember that."

Growing up, I didn't have much, but I was always well taken care of. For as long as I can remember, Mama Jean had been my guardian. She never wanted to tell me about my parents because she always felt like I wouldn't be able to forgive them if I were to ever encounter them again. Mama Jean is an older woman who says she was close to my father's family. When they found out about me, nobody wanted to take me in and raise me. She took me in with open arms. Though she wasn't the richest woman in the world, she made life work for us and I loved her with all my heart. When I turned 23, she was diagnosed with lung cancer and she didn't even try to fight it. I always told her she needed to quit smoking those cigarettes and her answer was always the same "I thought I was the mama round here, not you." I watched her go from the radiant woman I knew and loved to someone I could barely recognize. Six months after she was diagnosed, she passed. That was the hardest time of my life. Once she was gone, I fell into a deep depression and attempted suicide more than once. Sariyah and Marcellus were always there to save me and help me through every recovery. Though it took me a very long time to fully recover and realize Mama Jean would want me to live my life to the fullest, I vowed to live my best life.

Adonis: Hey beautiful. Hope you are enjoying brunch. Just thought about you

Me: Yup, we are tipsy and heading to dinner with her family

I decide to send him a selfie of me and my mimosa. Adonis is getting thumbs up but still I'm not on that type of time with a nigga that entertains bitches for fun.

As we are getting ready to leave, Sariyah is stumbling all over the place and I have to get myself together, so I can take care of her.

"Riy, you alright boo?"

"Yea Sin, I'm good, those 2 mimosas didn't do anything to me". She says laughing and then chugs what was her 7th mimosa.

"You mean 2 times 3 plus 1". I laugh as I hold her up against the table, we were seating at.

"Damn, I had that many. Well I had two and that's the story I am sticking to when Celly asks."

"Girl, he is gonna see as soon as we get out of that cab that you had more than 2."

I call the Uber. It's 5:30 and Aunt Lisa don't play about us being late to dinner. Since Sariyah decided to take full advantage of the unlimited mimosas at brunch, I have to get her to sober up before we got to the house. Even though they are both used to her getting wasted and professing her love for them at Sunday dinners, I don't want her walking in the house stumbling all over the place.

As the Uber pulls up, I can already tell this Uber driver is an asshole. He rolls down the window down, "Is she drunk?"

"No, I am not drunk. So please don't start the bullshit and unlock the doors." Sariyah yells at the driver.

We enter the Uber and I can see the driver looking in his rear-view mirror to make sure Sariyah isn't looking sick. For the whole ride, Sariyah is rambling about how much of a great friend I am and how much she loves all of us.

I am so thankful when we pull up to Aunt Lisa's house because she is no longer my problem. I am glad to hand her right off to Marcellus.

Marcellus

As I step out, walking down the steps, I laugh at Kaysin's face as she gets out of the Uber. I already know what time it is and how much I'm about to get in Sariyah's ass about getting wasted before Sunday dinner.

"She is all yours." Kaysin says after we parted ways from our hug.

"Celly baby, how are you?" Sariyah was good at holding her liquor but she has a few too many in her system. I know that Aunt Lisa is going to enjoy this when we get upstairs.

"I'm good, Princess. The real question is, how are you?"

"Come here." She places a kiss on my lips and whispers in my ear "I'm a little tipsy."

Though she is clearly drunk, I can't help but stare at her. She is so beautiful, and I know at this moment I am going to propose to her. I love her more every day with all her flaws and all the shit she puts me through, she still manages to keep a nigga happy.

I scoop her up and throw her over my shoulder.

"Celly, put me down, I'm feeling super dizzy."

Kaysin is laughing so hard that tears are coming out of her eyes.

I knock on the door, so Aunt Lisa can come and see what 's in store for her.

"Oh lord, Kaysin what the fuck was y'all drinking?" Aunt Lisa says as she slaps Sariyah on the butt.

"Auntie, I'm not passed out or drunk, Celly is just an asshole."
Sariyah yells as I put her down.

"She had one too many mimosas." Kaysin wraps her arms
around Aunt Lisa so tight while giving her a kiss on the cheek.
I appreciate my aunt for so many reasons. She is always there for me
especially after my mother just decided to up and leave me like I was
trash. She gave me a great life, and I was definitely spoiled growing up
and even now. So, the void I have to love and show affection is
something I always battle with for my own personal reasons. I am a
grown ass man who needs to step it up for the woman I love.

"Princess, let me holla at you for a minute." I grab her and take
her to my old bedroom.

"Marcellus, I already know why you dragged me in here, it's
not going down right now."

"Oh yes, it is, when we get home tonight you going to talk
about oh you have a headache and you need sleep."

"Not with Kaysin and Auntie down the hall."

"Oh please, this is not the first time we have done this."
Every time we had Sunday dinner at this house, we did it. At this point,
it is a ritual we must stick too.
As she undresses, I waste no time to do the same. Her body is so
amazing, and it takes me no time to stand at attention.

"Celly, make this worth my wild. I'm either going to sober up
or knock the fuck out on this bed."
We spent the next fifteen minutes taking over each other's bodies and
making the best of this quickie. It is more sensual when we have to be
quiet, we stare at each other with our best love faces.
Sariyah slips into the bathroom to fix herself and I walk back to the
living room as if nothing happened. We always thought if we appear at
different times, we were being real low key. Sariyah emerges from the
back shortly after with the biggest smile on her face.

"What y'all will do, is stop fucking every time y'all come over
here. I don't see any grand babies yet so y'all can wait until y'all get
home for all of that."

"We were not doing any of that."

"Bitch, yes you were with that stupid ass smile on your face."
Kaysin chimes in to take Auntie's side.

"Now you kids set the table, so we can eat, we have things to
discuss."

"I'm far from a kid, I'm a grown ass woman." Kaysin says as she flips her hair

"You better watch your grown ass woman tone, before I make you feel like a kid."

Something is different about Aunt Lisa today though. She has been acting funny since I got to the house earlier and I know she is up to something. She refuses to tell me. It has to be about the girls. I will never understand how my aunt can love everybody the way she does. She treats Sariyah and Kaysin as if she gave birth to them. I always wondered if me and Sariyah ever broke up, would my aunt turn on me or never allow me to bring anybody else home. It honestly makes me laugh out loud. Whatever this conversation is about, she knows we will listen to her ramble on like she always did. As long we have our fried chicken, macaroni and cheese, cornbread, collards, and her infamous chocolate cake, she can talk me to death. While Kaysin and Sariyah set the table, I feel like it is the right time to tell my aunt I am going to ask Princess to be my wife. I sit real close to her on the couch, so they can't hear me.

"Ma, I need to tell you something serious." The way she looks at me has me feeling real uneasy.

"Celly, you only call me Ma when it's real serious. Is Sariyah pregnant?" Her face beams every time she mentions those words.

"No, she ain't pregnant."

"Ain't nothing more serious than that boy.

"I'm going to propose, I think that more serious than a baby."

"FINALLY, it's about damn time."

Sariyah and Kaysin both look up and I know they about to be nosey.

"About time for what?" Sariyah said looking sad she was left out

"Celly is taking me out on a date, he has been so busy lately, he hasn't been treating me like I'm used to." Aunt Lisa has always been good at keeping secrets. "And that's the truth."

"We can spend a whole day as long as we can hit the mall to pick out a ring."

"You got a deal baby boy. I love you and I'm glad you finally want to step your game up. Now put a baby in her and we will be good!"

Aunt Lisa never had kids of her own. She is so happy to have me as her only child and can't wait until Sariyah and I have a baby. I'm sure she won't mind her having about 3 or 4 kids. They will all be spoiled all the time. We never have to worry about anything with my aunt, she is always there for all three of us.

As we all sit down, my aunt starts with prayer:

"Lord, thank you for the food we are about to receive. Thank you for blessing me with these beautiful human beings sitting at my table right now. All the blessings you have given them, I have noticed, and I thank you so much. Thank you for all the blessings you have given me. I haven't always been perfect but Lord you have put up with me and guided me in the right direction and lastly thank you for the ability to forgive and moving in the right direction. Amen."

"That was a deep and insightful prayer, Auntie." Kaysin says before I can even get the words out. "Which one of y'all fucked up? I'm all ears now because it ain't me."

"Alright now, just hear me out."

"I've always taught y'all to love and forgive. Kaysin even you. We aren't blood, but that really doesn't matter at this point. You and Riyah know my love is genuine, y'all also know what I believe in and how I feel."

I want her to get whatever the fuck is on her chest off right now. But I sit back and listen. She keeps looking at me but talking to everybody else.

"Riy, you are the perfect match for my baby boy. I know he is a handful, but you have shown him what love is and what it really means to love someone. He has opened up his heart in so many ways and I am thankful for you more than you will ever know."

She is on her emotional shit today. Something ain't right about this and I feel like she about to say some shit I don't want to hear.

"Celly, my king, you have grown into such a handsome young man. You have always been a gentleman and great to me. You were a big help around the house and you never caused me much trouble." She cries which I hate to see. "I know your mother wasn't sure about her decision, I'm guessing she did what she felt was right but I'm not mad that she left you at my doorstep. Actually, I thank God every day because I'm secure with knowing you grew into this amazing man."

"Thank you, Ma, I love you more than you know and stop calling that woman my mother."

So, this is what this forgiveness speech is about. This shit is about me.

"You need to let that hurt go Celly. She is the one that gave birth to you and raised you for 10 years."

"She barely raised me, if she wasn't up under some nigga, she was never home. I will never forgive her, but I'm no longer hurt about it. It is what it is." Getting frustrated, I adjust my chair and hold myself together. These women will not see how much this shit still affects me every day.

"So, you have no problem seeing her since you are no longer hurt."

When she says those words, I feel like I got hit with a ton of bricks and then another round came at me again before I can get an answer out.

"What do you mean see her, I haven't seen her in 18 years. 18 fucking years."

"She has been calling me Marcellus, begging me to let her see you."

"Get the fuck outta here, I don't want to see her at all."

"Celly, she is still your mother, hear her out." Sariyah makes direct eye contact with me.

"No disrespect to either one of you but fuck her and her stupid excuses as a mother."

"Boy, you better watch your mouth in my house and at my table."

"I said no disrespect Lisa, and I been here with you for the past week and you now telling me in front of them."

"You must have lost your damn mind boy. Go to your room and cool your ass down." She demands like I'm some child. "You got the right one today, that disrespectful shit ain't gonna fly in this house after all the shit I did for you."

"I'm sorry Ma, but God knows I can't forgive that woman." I get up to head to my room because I need a minute and she grabs me. I feel like a little ass boy running to her and shedding tears, but this shit is exactly what I never want to deal with.

Kaysin and Sariyah are both looking very uncomfortable and a little hurt by what I said. I can't control my temper whenever I get mad and can be very loose with my words.

"Maybe I should leave, this seems like a family issue." Kaysin says, trying to get up.

"Sin, my fault, you are family, I really didn't mean anything by what I said. Please stay. I'm gonna need a few shots after this news.

Seeing Marcellus break down like that really hurt my heart. When he snapped, I really wanted to jump over the table and slap him across his face for disrespecting Kaysin and I like that, but I know what kind of person I am dealing with. I really want to meet his mother for my own malicious reasons and give her a piece of my mind for abandoning my man the way she did. It will take a lot, but I am going to convince Marcellus to meet with his mother but not for all the right reasons. Our ride home is quiet. Though we had a few more shots before leaving and the tension between us is nonexistent, I know Celly still has the news on his mind and is weighing his options. He has a lot of unanswered questions and wants to the find out the truth. On the other hand, the truth hurts so maybe he will decide to just leave it alone. But, I won't.

"Princess, my bad about earlier." Marcellus approaches me from behind and kisses my neck. He knows that move right there gets me every time.

"I was about to get in your ass for disrespecting all of us, but I had to put my pride aside and put myself in your shoes for a minute." I turn around and rub his face.

"Baby, I don't know how to feel or what to do. This shit is so fucked up and I never thought about being around her again."

"Do you want to see her, or do you want to act like she never existed?"

"Part of me wants to see her to ask her all the questions I want answered and another part of me is like fuck her."

"Whatever you do, I support you and will be by your side."

"I know mama."

"You have a busy week this week, so let's leave this shit alone for a while, love you Princess."

"Love you Celly, I'm about to spend a few hours in my office so I am fully prepared for this hectic week."

I know he wants to be alone, and this is the perfect time for me to work. All that drama at Aunt Lisa's sobered my ass up and I am in full work mode with a little buzz. When I get in my zone, the magic I create is one of a kind. I can create a whole event sitting in front of the computer and just brainstorming. I use the same venues and vendors when planning something because I want to keep close relationships and need to trust nobody will fuck up any of my events. So far, so good. Jillian is my biggest client to date. This woman is making major bank, and she is giving and receiving major exposure on her social media. She is the CEO and founder of her own clothing line, J'Dore Clothing. She named the clothing line after her daughter J'Dore. I knew these two events had to be exquisite for two reasons. They are both personal events and she has repeatedly told me how much her children mean to her. Just like me, her major success has come within the last year. Her guest list has so many names of huge people in the industry. These events will be the talk of this year and I am so happy that my name will be on it.

I wake up to the sun shining on my face. I must've fallen asleep in my office. Last thing I remember was completing the agenda for the baby shower. I look at the time 8AM. How the hell did I sleep in this chair for that long? I didn't smell the aroma of breakfast, so I assume Celly is still asleep. I head toward my bedroom when I hear him talking out loud. I know I am wrong to be eavesdropping but what else should I do?

"Lord, life is just getting right where I need it to be. I'm about to ask the girl of my dreams to marry me and hopefully give her this baby she has been asking for. Honestly, I don't even know how the hell she puts up with my shit. My bad, Lord I can't help the cursing sometimes. Why did my mother have to come back and why does she want to see me? She hasn't given a fuck about me for the past 18 years. That's almost double the time of what she raised me. I really don't know what to do. Please, lord help me find a way. I need an answer."

Did he say he is going to propose? I shouldn't be eavesdropping on him but finally this is what I've been longing for. Now I wonder does he have a ring and when is he going to do it. Alright now, Riyah get it together. This is not about you, it's about him. I am beaming as I walk into the room. Luckily, his back is towards me, so time to wipe the big ass smile off my face or my cover is blown.

"Good morning, baby."

"You fell asleep in the office again, I was just about to come get you."

"I must have been tired, I haven't fallen asleep in the office in a long time."

"I know how much this gig with Jillian means to you, you are giving it your all."

"I'll make you some breakfast before I go to work babe. I'll whip up some French toast and sausage.

Now I see why he has been so attentive lately. He is ready to be a changed man and I'm here for it. I run water for my shower and call Kaysin to tell her the news. I can't keep my damn mouth shut.

"Bitch, guess what?" I didn't give Kaysin a chance to say hello.

"Girl, I haven't even open my eyes yet and bitch you sound like you been up for hours."

"I just woke up, but I overheard Celly talking to God."

"Run that again, talking to God." Kaysin said laughing. "I thought I was the only person who did that out loud."

"Yes, he does that from time to time but anyway he told God he was gonna ask me to marry him."

"Riyahhhhh, oh my god FINALLY bitch, yes I'll be your maid of honor."

"Girl, he didn't even ask me yet, actually he don't know I know. I've eavesdropped on his conversation with God." I whisper into the phone.

"Please don't do that again, I'm over here dying."

"I have to be patient and not be so obvious and I had to tell you that girl. I'm about to hop in the shower."

"Okay girl, I may stop by later tonight after work unless Adonis pulls up at my job which I'm low key hoping."

"Love you sis."

"Love you more."

I step into the hot water feeling like I'm floating on the clouds. As soon as he pops that question, I will not hesitate to say yes. I'm just waiting for him.

Kaysin

My girl is getting ready to be an engaged woman. I am so happy for her and she knows I can't keep a damn secret but who the hell am I going to tell. I know exactly who I can tell.

Me: Morning handsome

Damn, did I just cave and send a good morning text first? Riyah got me feeling the love in the air and now I am out here looking thirsty. That's the last thing I want to do.

Adonis: Good morning beautiful

I'm going to get my ass up and ready for work before I respond. Thank God Sariyah woke me up because I slept right through my alarm. All that shit that happened at Lisa's yesterday had my mind going crazy. I totally understand where Marcellus is coming from. I grew up without my mother and father. I have no idea where either of them are. Sometimes I wonder where they are and how could they not want to find me.

Even though it's Monday, I'm dressing like it's Friday. I am like 10 minutes from being late. My lavender blouse goes well with my high waist black jeans and my Louboutin's. Yes, I own a few pairs that are my favorites.

I jump in my car, no time for morning coffee.

Me: Running late for work, I had a crazy yesterday, really wanted to sleep in this morning.

The 20-minute drive to my job seems to take forever. I slide into the office without my boss seeing me.

"Morning Kaysin, 10am meeting with the team and 1pm phone interview with a potential manager for the new store opening in Yonkers." My assistant Myah is always on point. She is my prodigy. I'm prepping her to take my position when I finally leave this place. Don't get me wrong, I love my job, but I hate working under someone. Even though I have a high-ranked position, my boss Kyle Green is a sexist pig who feels like a black woman shouldn't be in my position. We continually bump heads and he always tries to belittle me.

"Look who showed up for work today on time," Kyle says entering my office without knocking.

"Am I not always on time?" Today I am not with the shits.

"Kaysin darling, actually, you are never late. You must get up at 6am to get here by 9am."

"Kyle, why would I get up at 6am when I live 20 min away."

"You know how you woman are, taking hours just to throw something on and come into work."

"How us women are, such a way with words. What's the agenda for the 10 o'clock meeting?"

"You will find out at the meeting, don't be late." He says shit just to get under my skin, so I have to clap back.

"Surprised you even have an agenda, since I'm always picking up the slack."

"Oh Kaysin, you can never pick up my slack, only a man can handle my job. Meeting is in Conference Room 4."

"Stupid ass." I mumble under my breath as soon as he walks away.

My phone vibrates.

Adonis: Been up since 6 checking the books for the barbershop. Hope you have a good day. Can I come scoop you later?

Me: Yes hun, I may need a drink or two.

Adonis: Damn, you having that kind of day already

Me: Yea, my douche ass boss tried me soon as I got through the door.

Adonis: I'll be there at 5

Adonis put a smile on my face instantly. Jayceon never came to my job when I was having a bad day. Working with Kyle I at least 2 unbearable days a week, he won't let me be great.

5 o'clock couldn't have come faster. After my encounter with Kyle, he tries to call me out in the meeting, but I am fully prepared for all his

questions. Myah got her hands on a copy of his agenda since his careless ass leaves everything out in the open in his office. My phone interview with the potential manager went great and I grant her a follow up in person interview.

"Hello beautiful."

"Oh my god, what the fuck are you doing here?" My day can't get any worse.

"You aren't happy to see me." Jayceon says as he approaches me with open arms.

"What part of leave me the hell alone don't you get?"

"Sin, in the 5 years we were together, how many times did you tell me that and didn't mean it?"

"Well, we aren't together, and I mean it."

I'm looking around to make sure Adonis isn't in the area. This is not looking too good.

"What are you looking around for?"

"I'm waiting for someone, nosey motherfucker."

"Another nigga, Sin, you got another nigga picking you up from work?"

"Jay, that's none of your business, now can you please leave?"

"Hell no, who is this nigga we waiting for, he gotta know you are off limits.

"Yea, she is off limits." Adonis appears out of nowhere. Lord have mercy on his fine ass coming to my rescue like Superman.

"Adonis let's go, don't even worry about him."

"Don't worry about me, that's how you treat your man of 5 years."

"You aren't my man."

"So, this is your man," Jayceon keeps looking at Adonis.

"No, he isn't my man either."

"Nah, I'm not her man yet but believe me that will change soon enough."

"Nigga please, you aren't getting what's mine."

"I am not yours."

"Jayceon my nigga, you cheated and lost your chance so let her go."

Out of nowhere, Jayceon punches Adonis in the face.

"Nigga, you don't fucking know me. Bitch, you told him my name."

"Who the fuck you think you talking to."
Adonis rubs his face but has this big grin on his face. He lunges towards Jayceon and beats the shit outta him. I'm in shock. I stand there frozen, not knowing what to do. So much going on my mind right now. Good thing I left the office before anybody else, this is so embarrassing.
Adonis kicks Jayceon in the ribs while he is on the ground.

"Don't you ever disrespect her or any woman in my presence."

"This shit ain't over, I got you."

"Sin, leave your car here and ride with me. I'll bring you back here tonight or pay for your Uber to work tomorrow."
I know that I have some explaining to do so I just follow him to the car. He gets in and starts the car without saying a word. We ride in silence until he pulls in the parking lot of the mall. I didn't even realize where we were going.

"Sin, what the fuck was that?"

"I came out of my job and he was standing there."

"Does he always talk to you like that?"

"Nah, he has never called me out of my name that caught me by surprise too."

"Listen, I'm gonna make sure he doesn't bother you anymore."

"How did you remember where I work?"

"The night at my crib, you told me a lot of things about work and your boss and that fuckboy."

"Oh, my goodness, I ramble a lot when I've had a few drinks."

"I'm about to cop a few things, spending bread is one of my coping mechanisms for my anger. We can grab some eats after I blow off this steam by blowing these bands. My fault, you had to see that shit, hopefully that's the last time."

"Shopping, food, and ready to throw the hands if needed, where have you been all my life?"
This day has been one hell of a day. I am so happy Adonis was there to save me even though everything was a shit show. He was not playing when he said he likes to spend money. We shop in damn near every store in the mall. He purchases a few things out of my normal shopping budget and wouldn't stop with his offers to buy me something, but I decline. I am not that kind of girl.

Adonis

I didn't think I would be fighting niggas over Kaysin already. It hasn't even been a week and I already have to lay her ex out. Not that I have a problem with it, and he will not be a problem much longer. There a few things I haven't told her yet. She has no idea who I really am in the streets and how I can just spend 2500 dollars in the first twenty minutes of being in this bitch. My barbershop was my father's business, he handed it down trying to convince me to get out the streets. Unfortunately, the little change it brings in doesn't pay all my bills, the shop's bills, and expensive necessities. So, I went from standing on the corner to becoming a businessman. In the basement of my barbershop is where my real business happens. I like to call myself a distributor. But the hood knows me as the king in these streets. I give people what they need, and they flip it for their own profit. Everyone speculates how much bread I'm really bringing in, that's why the Feds not on me. They never can find anything that would stick to my name. Before I put Sin on to my real hustle, I gotta make sure she is a down ass chick.

I offer to buy her a Gucci belt, but she declines. I don't give a fuck about her saying no, I bought it anyway. Money is never an issue for me. I spend it and make it right back.

"Adonis, I am getting hungry now. You can do this shit all day," Kaysin laughs.

She grabs a few things but insists on using her card. Every time we got to the counter, I make the cashier refund the transaction and swipe. I don't fuck with my cards much, so I gave it some activity today. I didn't want Sin to know how much cash I had on me.

The smile on her face has me tripping. She is everything I want in a woman, and she got her own money, not worrying about what's in my pocket.

"Adonis, is that you?"

Not today, this is not the time for it. I had to whip out this nigga. I don't need Kaysin getting into anything. I'm just going to ignore her and keep walking.

"Adonis, she is calling you." Kaysin looks at me and rolls her eyes.

"Adonis, I know you heard me." Shanell comes walking towards us and stops right in front of me.

"What's up Shanell?"

"It's been a minute since you hit my line, I see you been a little busy."

"Shanell, don't start your shit please."

"Sweetie, you not the only one believe me. Adonis here gets around quickly."

"Hun, I am not worried about anybody but myself." Kaysin on her shit.

"Adonis, hit me when you take her home."

"But what you not going to do is disrespect me while I'm standing here. He won't be hitting your line tonight or any other night."

"Like I said, Adonis hit me."

"I'm not gonna repeat myself again, you heard me the first time, so don't sit by the phone because it won't be ringing. Adonis babe, give me your phone."

I don't know what she is about to do. But I'm already turned on by her standing up to Shanell. She is looking at me like if I don't do as I am told I can kiss any future with us goodbye. I take my phone out, unlock it and hand it to her. She stands next to Shanell.

"Let's see, contacts, let's find your name Shanell, oh sweetie there you are. Now let's block and delete your number. It's that easy. Now you have a nice night Shanell and you can say your final goodbye to bae, I mean Adonis."

Shanell says nothing, but she walks away looking heartbroken. I really feel bad for her because I can't help but laugh. Kaysin and I crack up so loud, we both watch her as she turns back around to look at us.

"Yo, you are wild girl."

"Nah, she played herself. I was going to let her live."

"I'm bae now and you coming home with me tonight."

"Oh, please Adonis that was for show, you will take me back to my car after you pay for dinner."

"Damn girl, I thought we officially became a couple. I had to whip your ex out, and you had to shut down Shanell."

"Adonis, I'm sure there is many more where she comes from and I'm not shutting down anymore, that's gonna be your job."

It was something about this girl that has me thinking I need to change my ways. She carries herself so well and never let her confidence level change no matter the situation. We decide on Olive Garden for dinner. Kaysin makes me feel so comfortable and her beauty is immaculate. She is gonna make a nigga fall in love.

My phone rings.

Fuck! I gotta take this call.

"Yo what's up?"

"Dons, you need to get here now, there is 10 stacks missing from the stash."

"Fuck you mean 10 stacks, I just checked the books this morning and everything was good."

"Bro, I put today earnings in the safe and I went to count it for shut down and 10 stacks ain't there."

"If I get there and you miscounted, I'm beating your ass." Kaysin is staring at me hard, ready to drill me with questions.

"Alright yo, I'm finishing up my dinner and I'll be there in a second."

"I know I'm not crazy, did you say 10 stacks as in 10 thousand dollars?"

"Sin, I really have to figure out with the fuck is going on, and yes 10 thousand dollars is missing from my place of business."

"What the hell we still sitting here for?" "Excuse me." Kaysin calls the waitress over. "Can you bring us wrappers to go and charge this card for the bill?"

"Oh, hell no, you are not paying for this bill."

The waiter is already walking away with her card.

"Adonis, there is 10 stacks missing and at this point you don't know where it is. I can pay the bill it's not that deep."

"At least put my card in your Uber account, so I can pay for the ride since I was supposed to take you back."

"I'll let you do that."

She handed me her phone, so I could input my card into her account.

"Sin, you a real one and I promise I'll make it up to you."

"Adonis, it's not that big of a deal. We had an amazing time shopping and dinner was good just cut a little short."

I damn near knock the whole table over getting up to give her a hug and a kiss on the forehead. I really want to kiss her on the lips, but I respect that she isn't ready for that. The last woman I kissed was my daughter's mother. A shorty or two has caught me slipping on a drunk night. I don't even think about kissing bitches on the lips. One thing I know for sure, Kaysin ain't no bitch. She ain't ready for none of that shit, anyway. I saw how that crazy nigga was looking at her and I know she isn't dealing with any more bullshit. I don't even know what the fuck I'm feeling, let me get the fuck outta here.

"Text me when you get home."

I run out of Olive Garden so fast. If money is missing, they got me fucked up. Nobody ever messes with my cash and only 3 people have the safe code. Me, my shop manager, and my best friend Trey. The whole time driving to the shop my mind is running a mile a minute. I can't stop thinking about how Kaysin handled the situation with Shanel and me having to leave in the middle of our dinner. She was so perfect about it. She didn't ask a million questions or try to make a fuss about me leaving. She did the complete opposite. This really gotta be some catfish type of shit, but if not, I think I found exactly what I been missing.

Pulling up to the shop, I take a deep breath and pray I don't lose my shit.

"Wassup boss."

"Don't wassup boss me, I about to lock y'all all in here if I don't find my fucking money."

Walking downstairs, Trey is there counting the money, and he looks stressed.

"I counted this shit at least 5 times, I wanted to make sure you didn't have a reason to beat my ass. It's short."

I count the money with him and once we were both finish; I am livid. Someone booked me for 10 stacks and this shit never happened before. I'm not a killer but somebody is fucking with me on a personal level and I'm not afraid to bust my gun if needed. So, by any means necessary, I will find out who did this.

"What are we going to do?" Trey asks me after sitting there for a while. We came up with so many different scenarios.

"I don't fucking know, Trey."

There are so many things going through my mind now I'm not telling Trey because in my eyes he is the number one suspect. Trey and I have been best friends for almost 15 years now. He always did shady shit to other people, but I put up with him because he is like my brother. We met in middle school and lived in the same building for a long fucking time. My mother and father treated him like he was their own. He spent every holiday with us and his mother let him stay with us most of the time. She is a single mother and Trey is her only child. She would leave him in the house by himself a lot while she worked her overnight job. Trey knew his mother's schedule like the back of his hand, so he would sneak out and steal from everybody in the neighborhood. One night he tried to steal my mom's purse but when she realized it was him, she helped him instead of hurting him. Ever since that day, he would spend the night at my house when his mom worked, and my mother made sure he had a hot dinner every night.

I want to think this nigga was as loyal as I was to him but now I'm questioning this nigga's actions. He knows he can just ask me, and I will gladly give it to him. I was just in the safe and it wasn't short.

"Trey, let me ask you something."

"What's good bro?"

"Did you take the 10 stacks out the safe?"

"Are you fucking serious? Hell no. I didn't take that money from you."

"Alright, I just had to ask."

"Yo, you trippin. I'm out. You figure that shit out yourself."

"I'll see you later."

That nigga was out too quick, and he thinks I'm fucking stupid.

Kaysin: I'm home Adonis. Let me know if we have to ride out to get that 10 stacks back lol

Me: Nah shorty. That won't be necessary.

I already know who took my shit. Brothers or not, loyalty comes first.

Marcellus

This week has been crazy for Sariyah and I. She is going crazy about this event and my job has me pulling in long hours since it is the end of the first quarter. I been a bank manager for a year now and this has been the most fulfilling and stressful job I've had. The money is great, and I can say for 28, I am doing well.

"Good morning everyone. Our audit is coming up soon and I want to make sure everyone is on point."

"Marcellus, you know the team is strong and you manage the shit out of this bank. We haven't had any mishaps since you took the position." Corrine, a financial analyst said.

"Thanks, just keep up the good work. So, we can be prepared when they come in."

I walk into my office to go over all the paperwork one more time. This isn't my first audit, but I get nervous every time. Corrine enters my office and sits down across from me.

"Hey Celly, how you been? Since you got this promotion, you been super professional, or should I say just bougie."

"Don't call me that, It's Marcellus or Mr. Grant."

"Oh please, I been calling you Celly since I started here two years ago, and I see the way you look at me."

"Corrine, how do I look at you, like I want you to get some work done?"

Corrine has been making passes at me since she walked through the door. She is a beautiful female, but she don't got shit on Princess.

When I became bank manager, I stopped being friendly with her and became her boss. She was dating someone, but I am guessing it didn't work out between them two because she is all in my face again. I told Sariyah about Corrine on more than one occasion and promised her I would handle it but seems like she gonna have to handle this one.

"Ever since I walked into this bank, you have had your eyes on me but for some reason never took your chance."

"Two great reasons, my career and my lovely wife at home."

I can get used to calling her my wife. There is something about that shit that gets me hype.

"Oh please, there are so many niggas out there with wives and side chicks."

"Corrine, I ain't one," I walk over to my door and open it.

"Please make sure that all of your paperwork is ready for me by end of day."

"No problem, Mr. Grant."

Not only was this audit stressing me out, the thought of my mom trying to be a part of my life is weighing heavy on my mind. She can't possibly think seeing me would be easy and that I will accept her with open arms. I don't want to see her, but I want answers about her actions. My phone rings, and I know it's Sariyah checking in on me. She calls me at least three times a day, just to check on me.

"Hey Riyah, how are the finishing touches for tomorrow going?"

"Celly, I am so stressed and drained, but I keep telling myself it's all worth it in the end."

"Yes baby, it is well worth it."

"How is your day going?"

"You know this audit is coming up, so I am a little stressed and I got an office visit today."

"Celly, enough is enough. On Monday, I am coming to handle that bitch."

"Hold your horses, you don't even know what I'm talking about."

"Your whole voice changes when you think I am going to be mad at you, and she is the only thirsty bitch that tries to give your office visits on a regular."

I recognize my boss coming through the door with two other unfamiliar faces, which means it's time for my audit.

56

"Baby, baby I have to go, Jim is here with the bosses, they are probably here for the bank audit."

"Okay, love you and good luck."

"I love you too baby girl."

I almost hang up on her because I'm so nervous, but I ain't trying to be in the doghouse again.

"Hello Mr. Grant, it is that time again please set aside all paperwork and get your team ready for the yearly audit."

"Yes sir, whenever you are ready, we are fully prepared. I will be in the back by the vault."

It seems like they are in the bank forever and I'm sweating bullets. This is the first audit with me being first in command and I want to make sure everything goes well. My heart races as they interview every employee especially Corrine's sneaky ass. I know she isn't going to do anything to jeopardize both of our positions at the job.

"Mr. Grant, let's step into your office." Jim says as they wrap up the audit.

We enter my office and he shut the door.

"Marcellus, you have exceeded my expectations. I promoted you because I saw your potential, but your employees are airtight and professional. All your accounts and loans are current and looking good. I want to let you know I am very proud of you. I don't know if you know this, but you qualify for a two thousand dollar raise. So, congratulations and thanks for taking care of business always."

We exchange a firm handshake and he left with the other bosses. This is what I work so hard for. That recognition just reassures me I have my job down and the only way is up.

Sariyah

This last week has been the craziest week I've had in a long time. I spent the last few days paying all the vendors and people who would take part in the event. Jillian stuck to her budget and appreciated that I didn't ask her to raise it at all. She gave me an outrageous number for what she needed so I didn't even think about increasing it. It is now Friday, and I am so happy that the event is tomorrow and almost over with. Kaysin is spending the night with me because she helps me with every event I organize. I can't wait until I am making enough money to pay her what she deserves. Now she does it for free, well technically I pay her with my love.

"Riy, let's pop this bottle of champagne in celebration of completing all the preparation for this event and not pulling all your hair out." Kaysin pulls out a bottle of Moet and hands it to me.

"Yes, but only two glasses tonight. We have to be up at 8am to be out the house by 9."
Every time I pop a bottle, I just smile at my accomplishments.

"I know, it's the same routine every event. I got your back babe."
We stay up for a little while longer after downing the two glasses of champagne. My anxiety is not as bad as it used to be. This is my passion and I am so happy to be living my dream.

The next morning

"It's the big day Princess," Marcellus says while waking me up with kisses. "I made you a quick breakfast."

"Thanks, Celly." I hop out of bed and run to the kitchen. I have to get my meal in because I'll be too busy to eat.

Kaysin is already in the kitchen fully dressed and eating her breakfast. This is why I really fuck with her. This girl is always supporting me. Marcellus isn't far behind me as I settle down to eat.

"Morning sis, I told you I would be up. I have to do my makeup and hair." Kaysin said as she stood up "Is this appropriate for a 5th birthday party."

She had a beige blouse that wrapped around with a low v cut and high-waisted jeans. She literally can wear a sheet and it will look bomb on her.

"Yes, it's not too much." I say smiling "What shoes are you wearing?"

"My Gucci sneakers."

"Girl, I'm wearing mine too, you know those are the good luck charms."

"I remember when y'all literally saved up pennies for those sneakers. It was hilarious." Marcellus chuckles at the thought of the method to our madness.

Kaysin and I aren't flashy females by any means. We have always had expensive taste but couldn't always afford it. When I turned 25, we vowed to save up 10 dollars per week to put towards buying each other the same pair of Gucci sneakers. We could have easily bought the sneakers with our paycheck and would have been broke right after. We wanted to see if accomplishing saving money was something, we were capable of. We even made a piggy bank that read "Gucci Gang." After what seemed like forever, we took a trip to the Gucci store and paid for our sneakers with the same 70 tens we put in the piggy bank. It was a beautiful moment for the both of us. To think 3 years later, I can walk into a Gucci store and buy whatever I want and not think twice about what's in my bank account. I'm still balling on a budget with no shame in my game.

"Alright, girl. Put your makeup on and get that hair did. I know it will take you about an hour to do so we can get out of here."

"Meet back here." I put my hand out, and she places hers on top.

"Okay break."

We always play around when we are in high-stress situations.
Finally, we get the venue and when I tell you I am in awe by all that is
already here. The venue already has the tables set up with the décor.
The only thing left is designing the stage and where Jillian and her
family will be sitting. 3 hours left until Jillian shows up to drop off a
few things and come to see the space. The photographer and
videographer are here to catch her reaction.

After we set up everything, my eyes are filled with tears. I am so proud
of myself and you can see the growth in my work and designs. J'Dore's
name is spray painted on what looks like the wall but is actually a
removable sheer cloth. The décor is pink and white. She has a three-tier
cake, along with a candy bar and cotton candy machine. There is a
portrait of Jillian and J'Dore that they took for her maternity shoot
along with a picture of the whole family and then one of J'Dore alone.
On each table there is a Polaroid camera with a film of 25 pictures and
a photo booth.

"Riyah, this shit is off the meter." Kaysin screamed

"This has to be the best outcome thus far, especially for a kid's
party. You know this is a little out of my element."

"Boo, it's time to broaden your horizons and get to this paper."

My phone is vibrating, it's Jillian and my heart drops.

"Hello, Sariyah speaking."

"Hey Sariyah, I'm downstairs. I hope everything is ready."

"Of course, come right up and make sure to have your eyes
closed."

"Jason and Cliff, get ready she is coming up now." The
videographer and photographer quickly set up to get Jillian's reaction.
Jillian's husband is escorting her inside with his hands over her eyes.

"Hey Jill, are you ready to see what we have created?"

"Yes, I am so ready."

Her husband slowly removes his hand. Jillian looks around at
everything and doesn't say a thing. I am so nervous and scared. I know
deep down she loves it but when she says nothing; I get a little worried.
I take a final glance around the room to make sure everything is as
perfect as it was before she came in. I glance back at her and she is
crying.

"Sariyah, this is so beautiful. Oh, my god." She pulls me into a
hug so tight. I feel like I'm suffocating the baby. "Thank you so much.
J'Dore will love this."

"Jillian, you had me scared for a second."

"No honey, I was just speechless."

"Thank goodness. Let me introduce you to my assistant and best friend Kaysin."

"Hi, I'm Kaysin and I am at your disposal today. Whatever you may need, I am here to help."

"Thank you. I'm Jillian."

"You are carrying your pregnancy so well and you are glowing honey."

"Thanks, hun, she is behaving herself for her big sister because some days it is hard for me to get out of bed."

"Well, don't stress yourself too much today, we will make sure everything goes as planned."

"Thanks again. I'm going to drop some stuff off and head out to get myself and J'Dore ready for the party."

Kaysin and I are working our asses off for the next few hours. We do take a little break to take pictures in the photo booth. I will add it to the catalog of pictures that we have. Marcellus stops by to check out the venue and make sure I am good. He never stays for events because he says, "Don't want to knock you off your game, I will distract you with my handsome self."

As 3 pm approaches, guests arrive. The photo booth area is the first thing people experience and then they move along and are taken to their assigned tables. There are so many known artist and designers with their children. I stay at the front and introduce myself to as many people as I can. Jillian offered me the opportunity to network before she arrives with J'Dore and I damn sure take the chance. The guest of honor arrives with her parents and instantly steals the room. J'Dore is the cutest little thing and I want to squeeze her cheeks. I really want a baby of my own. Seeing Jillian with her family has me feeling someway inside. Marcellus needs to hurry with this engagement and baby. It quickly broke my thoughts when I see Jayceon walk in with a woman. I run over to Kaysin as fast as I can.

"Sin, look who just walked in the door.

Kaysin

I'm busy making sure all the guests have received their plates already and when Sariyah runs towards me like her last name is Bolt.

"Sin, look at the fucking door."

My heart stops when I see Jayceon and Asia. Sariyah has never met Asia, but she knows exactly who that heffah is.

"Sariyah, that's Jayceon and Asia."

"I recognized Jayceon trifling ass but, had no clue the girl was Asia."

"What the fuck are they doing here?"

"Girl, how am I supposed to know?"

We watch as J'Dore runs over to Asia to take a photo with her and Jayceon in the photo booth.

"Auntie Asia, what did you get for me for my birthday?"

"You just have to wait and see J."

I can't believe I am in the same space as Jayceon and this girl. I want to run out of the door, but I have to help my girl out. How the hell does this even happen? Small fucking world.

"Kaysin, get your shit together. They are walking this way."

I really don't want to cause a scene at this party, but I know Asia will get out of pocket. My first instinct is to fold my arms and stand my ground. I'm clueless on why I am still a threat to this girl. I gave her this nigga, and she took him with open arms. She needs to keep her dog on a leash because he keeps straying away from home.

"What the fuck are you doing here?" Asia wastes no time to approach me on her ratchet shit.

"I am here just helping a friend. Asia, this is my best friend Sariyah, she is the one who organized this party for your niece." I want things to be smooth because this is Riyah's event and we need this to be perfect.

"Hey Kaysin, you looking real good today." Jayceon says smiling and biting his lip.

I ignore him and address Asia.

"Asia, I don't want any issues with you. This is your niece's party."

"Bitch, you so lucky this isn't the time and place for me to address your ass."

Asia grabs Jayceon and walks over to greet Jillian and her husband.

That went better than I expect so thank you Jesus.

The party was so lit, and everyone had a good time. I'm thinking we are in the clear, all the guests are gone, and we are cleaning up. J'Dore already left to go home with another family member. It is still a few of us there.

"Kaysin, now I can address your ugly ass." Asia approaches me from behind as I'm folding up chairs.

Everyone in the venue turns to look at us.

"Whoa, this is still not the time and place." Sariyah jumps in between us.

"Shorty, this has nothing to do with you. Kaysin trying to look so innocent when she knows damn well she is still sleeping with my man."

"Excuse me, Asia nobody wants his cheating ass." I yell out at her "Why are you mad anyway, he been a cheater since you met him. Did you forget?"

"Bitch please, that nigga never acknowledged you and always told me I was number one in his life."

"Well, good for you so I'm trying to figure out why you still pressed about me."

"Ain't nobody pressed."

"You can never be me Asia, Jayceon still begging me to let him back in. He came to my job the other day and my man beat his ass."

"And now I am about to beat yours."

Asia lunges at me and punches me in my face. That's the only hit she gets in. I'm not letting up. I wish she would have learned her lesson the first time. When I dragged her naked body out of my bed and whipped her ass. Poor little Asia don't want this problem. I completely black out for a minute. I finally came back to reality when I feel someone pulling me off of her.

"Jillian, I am so sorry, but that bitch had it coming." I say to Jillian as soon as I can get myself together.

"I'm going to kill you, watch your back Kaysin," Asia screams as Jayceon drags her out of the venue.
Jillian just looks at me and laughs so hard. Sariyah and I look at each other, we can't help but laugh either.

"Honestly, I can't stand her stupid ass. That's my husband's sister, and she is always looking for a problem or in a problem," Jillian says rubbing her belly still laughing. "Kaysin, you have a set of hands on you."

"I try not to use them anymore, but Asia needed a good ass whipping."

"If you don't mind me asking what's her beef with you."

"Please let me answer this." Sariyah speaks up. "Jayceon was Kaysin's man for three long ass years and then Asia decided she wanted them to share him. She got caught in the bed Jay and Sin shared. Kaysin packed his shit and gave him to Asia to keep but Jayceon still obsesses over Kaysin so that's why we are here now."

"Oh damn, you are Jayceon's ex she is always talking about, that girl hates you and I'm pretty sure you make her insecure." Jillian makes me smile when she says Asia always talks about me. I'm not self-centered but to think this bitch really gives me all this energy makes me laugh, she is really that bothered by me.

I decide to text Adonis about the events. I haven't gotten a chance to look at my face, but she did hit me hard and it's stinging.

Me: Got in a fight with Jayceon's girlfriend

Not even a second past.

Adonis: WTF?! Where are you? I'm on my way

I send him the address to the venue. I'm not sure if I'm ready for Sariyah to meet Adonis, but I guess it's happening tonight, or I can just tell him to wait in the car.

The men have taken over the cleaning since Asia's fiasco turned into girl talk.

"Adonis is on his way. He is probably shook since I told him I had a fight with Asia."

"Can I meet him?" Sariyah gave me the eye saying, "I am going to meet him."

Adonis: I'm here.

He got here so quick. I have to mentally prepare myself for this meeting, but I guess we have to go in blind.

"Riy, he is here and please be nice."

"I promise I will be nice, let me say good night to Jillian." She walks over to the rest of the family. Jillian hands her an envelope and waves goodbye to me.

"What's in the envelope?" I said jokingly. I wanted her to tell me, I'm so nosey.

"Girl, I don't know. She told me to open it when I get home." My heart is racing so fast as we walk down the steps. Adonis meeting Sariyah is a big deal. I didn't give him warning just to see how he would react. This just turned into a setup. I see his car sitting right in front. He hops out as soon as he sees me.

"Sin, are you okay?" Adonis pulls me into a hug so tight "Baby girl, your eye is black and blue, what the hell happened?"

"I'm good, she looks way worse than I do." "Adonis, this is my best friend Sariyah."

"Hey, I heard so much about you, nice to meet you." Adonis held his hand for her to shake it.

Sariyah put her hand in his and smiled.

"Hey, is she telling the truth?"

"About what?" Sariyah asks confused.

"About ol' girl looking worse than her."

"Oh yea, definitely, Kaysin is Mayweather Jr."

"Nah, actually I didn't," Adonis laughs. "I'm going to take her back to my place if you don't mind."

"She is all yours, please take care of her she has been on her feet all day."

"Believe me, I will."

Sariyah pulls me to the side and I already know she will either say run for the hills or that she approves.

"Girl let's hope this is the one, he was so attentive to you and he is nice." Sariyah smiles and gave me a hug. "I approve."

I hug her with everything in me and run to the car.

"Call me when you get home Riyah, Love you" I yell back towards her as I walk to the car. Adonis is ready to talk my ear off. "Love you too Sin.

Adonis

When I got that text from Kaysin, I dropped everything I was doing and hopped in the car to head straight to her. My first thought was why the hell is she fighting Jayceon's hoe, but I will find out later. I pull up to the address she texted me. I know today is that event with her friend so I'm guessing this is where she's at. I pull my piece out just in case that nigga Jayceon is still around. I don't want Kaysin to see that side of me, but I have to protect me first. As soon as she comes out the door, my heart stops. Her eye was bloodshot red with black and blue marks around it. Everything else looks good, but her eye is looking crazy. Damn, I'm feeling her. Last time I seen her was when I bounced at dinner, but we been texting and talking on the phone and she is real. I get out the car and the first thing I did was give her a snatch her into to my arms and examine her eye. I see her friend standing there, but I didn't really care to introduce myself until I know Kaysin is good. Kaysin introduces us and her friend is cool. My mind is only on one thing, getting her back to my house. We say our goodbyes and I head back to the car. They are talking about me, women love to gossip. As soon as Kaysin's ass gets in this car, I'm asking her a million questions.

"Hey boo, you didn't have to come get me." Kaysin says as she gets in the car.

"Cut the shit, don't hey boo me. Why the fuck are you fighting in these streets like some hoodrat?"

"First of all, it wasn't in the streets, it was in the venue and she punched me first, so I whipped her ass."

"Kaysin, don't be smart, what the fuck happened for real?"

She breaks the whole story down and all I could say was "Small fucking world."

"Same thing I said, I need to ice my eye before it swells."

"We heading to my crib now."

The rest of the ride is quiet. Kaysin falls asleep as soon as we pull off and I catch myself staring at her. She is still beautiful even with her black eye. Her hair is up in a messy bun with bangs in her face. I pull up to my apartment complex. The luxury of living in a penthouse, parking spot on deck. I park the car and sit there for a minute.

"Baby girl, we here." I say nudging Kaysin to wake up.

"Damn, I fell asleep, it was a long ass day."

"I can tell, now let's get you upstairs and ice that eye, Blackey."

"Shut up."

She has me ready to ice her eye and her whole body. I thought this relationship shit wasn't for me, but she got me looking at shit differently. All these females on my dick ain't gonna make it easy but, shit it's gotta happen.

We get in the house and I am so happy to be home. The fucking shop has been my home since I figured out Trey stole my money. I gotta sleep with one eye open guarding my goddamn safe. Trey's bitch ass hasn't called or came by the shop since I accused him of stealing, that nigga always been a stupid ass. I don't even care about the money that shit don't mean nothing. It was the principle that my brother stole from me.

"Adonis, get me a washcloth and towel please" Kaysin says "I need to take a shower and ice my eye."

"It's in the bathroom next to the shower."

"Thank you."

This girl is getting in the shower and I want to get in there with her. It is the longest 20 minutes I ever. While she is in the shower, I make her a homemade ice pack and grab some cocoa butter, so I can nurse her back to health.

"That shower was so good."

I turn around and drop the ice pack on the floor. She has on a Nike sports bra and Nike leggings, but from where I'm standing, she is butt ass naked.

"KAYSIN, where are your clothes?" I yell.

"I am fully clothed, silly. I wear this to the gym all the time."

M. LaShone

"Not no more, my girl wears sweat suits to the gym."

"Adonis, what I been telling you, second to no one."

"Sin, I'm working on it."

"That's a shame, you have to work on getting rid of these bitches."

"I am a single man, what you want me to do?" I sat down next to her and put the ice pack on her eye.

"It's pretty bad right?"

"Yes, but you are still beautiful, that shit will go away."

"Adonis, who decorated your crib, this shit is nice."

"I already know what you thinking, shows you don't know shit about me, we gonna change that."

"What I am thinking?"

"One of my hoes decorated, but actually I decorated every room in the house."

"I am impressed."

"Tell me two facts about you and I will tell you two facts about me, since clearly you don't know me well enough."

"Okay, my mom or dad gave me up at birth and was raised by a family friend who passed away a little while ago because no one else wanted me." Kaysin says with her head down.

"Wow, sorry to hear that."

"Nothing to be sorry about, Mama Jean was the best mother and father I could ask for."

"My daughter is 6 years old." I blurted out before she finishes her sentence.

This is the best time to drop this bomb on her since she dropped her shit on me. She took everything else so well. She is either going to throw this ice pack and leave me for good or let me wife her ass up. I kept Anais a secret because she is sacred. I don't put my business out there to just anybody but, Kaysin ain't just anybody.

"Oh wow, now that's a little lady I can't compete with. Didn't I just tell you I come second to none?" She said laughing "Let me see baby girl."

I open my phone and pull up pictures of my daughter.

"Are you mad I didn't tell you?"

"Why would I be mad, we getting to know each other. We both have a past and we can't change what's already happened. To be

69

quite honest, I don't want to. It made us who we are today," Kaysin smiles. "Tell me more about her."

"She lives with her moms upstate, but she comes to the city every summer and all her vacations. Her moms and I try to co-parent as best we can even though sometimes I can't stand her ass."

"So, this Christmas, I will meet her."

"If you are still around."

"I'm sure I'll still be around."

"Fact number 2 Sin."

"I can sing my ass off." She says laughing

"Oh shit, you lying, let me hear something."

"Some people want it all, but I don't want nothing at all. If it ain't you baby if I ain't got you, baby. Some people want diamond rings and some just want everything, but everything means nothing. If I ain't got you, you."

She stares at me as she sings these words, like she really means that shit. I can't control myself. I lean in and kiss her. I haven't kissed a female in so long. That is something intimate you can't go around kissing every female. I don't go down on any female and I don't kiss them on the lips unless I know she is only mine and I trust her. I been wanting to kiss Kaysin since we sat at dinner that night at Ricardo's. To my surprise, she didn't stop me. I remove her clothes and next thing I know she is on top of me.

"Fact number two Kaysin, I like you & I want to make love to you." I feel like a bitch but looks like it's working.

I carry Kaysin to my room and we explore each other's bodies like never. I place her down on my bed and rip her leggings off. She isn't wearing anything under.

"Oh, so you knew this was about to go down." I laugh

"Shut up and eat this pussy." Kaysin threw herself back and I show her everything she has been missing

"Oh shit, right there, don't stop." Kaysin screams with pleasure. I push her legs all the way back and went to work.

"Damn, you so wet and tight." I pull my dick out ready to enter her body. She jumps up and makes me disappear.

The way she moves her mouth around my dick makes me want to explode right now. Fuck, I know I ain't going to last.

She does tricks I have never seen in my life and I've had my share of women. My knees buckle, and I have to stop her.

"Bend your ass over."

Kaysin bent over in front of me and climbs back on the bed. I enter her body and she screams in ecstasy. My dick is so hard, this nut is about to take the life out of me.

I'm giving her the best 10 minutes of her life and by the looks of it, it completely satisfies her. She already dozing off.

"Oh no, that is only round one. Get that ass ready for the rest of the night."

She let me kiss every inch of her body and she does the same to me. We were at each other all night and I already knew she wasn't going anywhere.

The sun was shining in my room as I roll over, I see Kaysin's naked body next to me. She is the first woman in my bed. I always met bitches I was dealing with at their cribs. I don't want no stalkers or crazy girls popping up at my crib. Last night got a nigga fucked up and, she better not hop out this bed and try to run. Her fine ass is mine now.

Sariyah

After telling Marcellus about the events at the birthday party, we just lay in bed and laugh at all the stress we have been dealing with these past few weeks. The news about his raise has me ecstatic. He works so hard and deserves to be rewarded. This week has been a money changer for the both of us. A few weeks ago, I was ready to leave his ass. Who the hell am I fooling? I'm in this thing for life. Career wise, we are set. I know Marcellus is still thinking about his mom and the reality sets in that my mother is no better than his. Only difference is she has been in my life constantly. I wish my relationship with her was different but, my mother is so stubborn. I have to worry about my life and building my family. The rest will happen when it does.

"Corrine don't want to see me, Marcellus."

"Princess, I know, somebody need to whip her ass, but I really don't want to come to that."

"You need to fire her ass."

"She is a great employee though and I have no means to fire her."

"How about sexual harassment, don't let that shit happen again."

"Doesn't it feel good just too lay in the bed with nothing to do but cuddle and talk shit?"

"We about to be on our Netflix & Chill, let's order food, you don't have to cook tonight."

"Riyah, when you gonna start cooking for me?"

"Celly please, before we moved in together, you knew I couldn't cook," I say laughing "Don't try to switch on me now, you are the chef of the house."

"I am the man of the house, a king on his throne."

"Yea, that cooks for the queen."

I climb out the bed to get the envelope Jillian gave me at the end of the birthday party. She told me not to open it until I get home. It's a gold glittered envelope that said Thank You.

"Celly, Jillian gave me this after the party."

When I open it, my mouth falls open.

"It's 5,000 dollars in here." I scream as I count the money out loud, throwing the bills on the bed. I count it like 5 times to make sure I'm not crazy. I immediately call her.

"Hey Sariyah." Her voice sounds as if she knows exactly what I am calling her for.

"Jillian, I can't take this money from you, you paid me for my services already."

"It's a tip. I told you to open it at home because I knew you would try to return it."

"Thank you so much Jillian, it has been a pleasure working with you and the baby shower will be a movie."

"Oh god, please no, J'Dore keeps talking about her party, let's cancel the shower." She says laughing.

"Nope, you already have everything secure."

"See you soon."

Marcellus is still staring at all the money I threw on the bed.

"Sariyah baby, it's official you about to blow up baby.

Since Adonis graced my life with his presence, everything has been blissful between us. We aren't in a relationship yet, but we make it clear to each other that we want to be exclusive. I been busting my ass at work. We all know shit doesn't change. Kyle makes my job harder every day and I still want to give him my ass to kiss. Honestly, I am working towards taking his position and getting his ass fired. Today is a typical day in the office until there is a knock on my office door.

"Hey Kaysin, this came in for you." Myah walks in with 2 dozen red roses.

"Oh my god, these are so beautiful." I run towards her and grab the flowers.

"Sweet lady, would you be my sweet love for a lifetime?" - Adonis read the card attached to the flowers.

I immediately pick up the phone to call him and to my surprise, he doesn't answer. Adonis answers all my calls. So, I call 10 more times and still I get no response. I go from the happiest woman in the world to the angriest woman in the world that quick. How did he expect me to be his lady and he can't even after the damn phone? I need to calm down before I go crazy. I dial Sariyah's number so fast.

"Hey boo, how is your day going?" Sariyah answers on the first ring like Adonis was supposed to.

"Adonis sent me flowers asking me to be his girlfriend and now that nigga is not answering the phone."

I am livid and holding back tears. Adonis has learned so much about me in the time we spent together, and he knows I'm not with the shit.

"Kaysin, he is probably busy at work and doesn't have his phone on him."

"Adonis always has his phone on him and he always answers."

"Kaysin, he has spoiled you rotten if you think that man is supposed to answer every call you make."

"Maybe not the first one, but after the tenth call, his ass should know to answer the phone. It could be an emergency."

"Honey, you sound like I did when Celly and I started dating." Sariyah laughs and that pisses me off even more. "That man has a business to run and has room to not answer your call without you assuming the worse."

"I haven't even thought the worse yet, what if he is with another woman like his last hooray before he settles down?"

"Girl, you are talking crazy from what you tell me, he worships the ground you walk on."

"He does, well he acts like he does."

"Actions speak louder than words, Kaysin, give him a break."

"You are right, Riyah."

"Now sis, I got to get back to work. Love you and call me later."

Sariyah calms me down a lot and I guess I have been a little spoiled. Adonis is at my beck and call anytime I need him. We rarely talk during work hours, so he can just be busy. I grab my flowers and kiss the card he sent me. I'm heading home and wait for my man.

As soon as I get home, I take all my clothes off and run a bubble bath. A woman always needs to have her "me time". There is a knock at my door and I run to the door in excitement. Without thinking twice, I swing the door open, but my smile quickly turns to a frown.

"Jayceon, what are you doing here?"

"Kaysin, you really thought I would leave you alone."

"You have left me alone."

"No, I let you think I did, I've been watching you."

"What the hell do you mean, you have been watching me.?"

"Every day Kaysin, I see you with him every fucking day."

I am terrified. I have never seen Jayceon this angry in all the years we were dating. He looks like a completely different person. I'm focusing on keeping my towel up and getting him the hell out of my house. He walks over to the table and grabs my flowers after reading the card; he flings the flower vase across the room.

"You will never be his because you will always be mine." Jayceon lunges towards me and grabs my neck

"Jay, let me go, please."

"Stop telling me to let you go and stop telling me to leave you alone." He squeezes tighter making it almost impossible for me to breathe.

"I CAN'T BREATHE."

"Now you know how it feels, how it feels to not breathe. I can't function without you Sin. I've been drinking and fucking bitch after bitch and none of them do what you did for me."

He finally lets me go and I fall to the floor.

"Jayceon, you know you fucked up. We can never be together again."

He slaps me so hard and busts my lip. It's bleeding so bad. My phone rings but I can't get to it. He keeps hitting me like I'm a stranger on the street. I give up. I don't have the strength anymore. I never thought he would put his hands on me.

"Kaysin, you know you will always be mine and now you trying to be with another nigga."

My towel falls, and I crouch into a fetal position trying to protect my face and body.

"Jayceon, you are scaring me."

"Sin, now you fear me. Look at you and your beautiful body."

He kisses me, and I get up the courage to punch him in the face.

"Bitch, you just punched me." Jayceon punches me back. I give up. I feel so defeated. I never thought he would put his hands on me.

"Get out now!"

"Not until you give me what I want."

He picks me up and throws me on the couch. I kick and scream as much as I can, but his strength is overpowering me.

"Stop Jayceon STOP!"

I'm crying and screaming, with my eyes shut tightly. I can't bear looking at him anymore.

Jayceon just stops suddenly and I squint my eyes open to see if he is still over me.

Adonis is standing there with a gun pointed at Jayceon's head.

"Nigga, you can thank my girl for me not blowing your fucking brains out right here." Adonis' voice gives me chills. "Just know your days are numbered because this is where you fucked up."
He slaps him with the butt of his gun and knocks two of Jayceon's teeth out.

"Get the fuck out."
Jayceon looks like he wants to say something, but the blood leaking out of his mouth is preventing him from saying anything. He stumbles out the door.

"Adonis, where were you?" I can't stop crying and he holds me tight.

"Baby girl, I'll explain everything to you later. We have to get you to the hospital.

When I walk into Kaysin's building, I already know she is going to kill me. She called my phone about 15 times, but I couldn't answer. I was having a meeting with my shop manager Shawn about Trey. I haven't seen Trey since the night I accused him of stealing the 10 stacks from me. Shawn informed me that Trey still coming to the shop when it opens and going in the safe. I been so wrapped up in Kaysin, the shop been the last thing on my mind. Shawn is first in command and holds shit down. Everything was cool until that motherfucker Trey started popping back at the shop telling him he is coming to pick up money and bringing it to my crib. Shawn doesn't question him. It slipped my mind to even tell him what the fuck was going on because I wanted to handle this shit on my own. It still has me tripping because he been robbing me blind. My dumbass didn't even realize it. Trey's snake ass gotta go.

As soon as the meeting was done, I ran to Kaysin's house. I know baby girl got my flowers and I'm ready to tear her up and make her forgive me. When I make it upstairs and see her door cracked open, I immediately pull my gun out. I hear her screaming and crying. I'm ready to shoot the whole shit up.

I walk into her apartment and this nigga is on top of her. I almost pull the trigger with no second thought until Kaysin's weak and fragile body caught my eye. This shit can't go down how I really want it too. I press the gun against that nigga's head and say my peace. After I bust his fucking mouth open, he knows what time it is. Seeing my shorty fucked

up has me seeing red. I'm already pissed about Trey's bitch ass and now this nigga. Today is a bad fucking day.
I have to get Kaysin to the ER and doing 100 on the highway to get her to the hospital is the only option.

"Baby, I am so sorry." I plead to her

"He has been watching us, stalking us."

"What?"

"He told me he has been watching us and I can never be yours, and I will always be his." Kaysin says crying hysterically.

"Baby, calm down, I got you and you are mine. Just like I was there to protect you today, I will always be there to protect you."

"Thanks baby." Kaysin keeps drifting in and out.
When I pull up to the hospital, I try to waking her up, but she isn't moving up.
I panic and carry her to the emergency room.

"My girl passed out, someone beat her up."
The nurses come rushing me and grab her out of my hands.
It seems like I'm waiting out there for hours. A phone keeps ringing, but I don't recognize the ringtone. Oh shit, it's Kaysin's phone. Sariyah's name pops up.

Fuck!

"Hello."

"Who is this?"

"Hey Sariyah, it's Adonis."

"What's wrong?" Sariyah yells. "Where is Kaysin?"

"We are at the hospital."

"What hospital?"

"New York."
Before I could get another word out, the phone disconnects. This is too much shit going on for one day.
Sariyah comes flying through the door with an older woman and a man. She spots me as soon as comes into the waiting room.

"Adonis, what happened to her."

"Jayceon beat her up and tried to rape her."

"Have you seen her?"

"Yea, I bought her here, she was unconscious when they took her to the back. That was about an hour ago."

"What's good man, I'm Marcellus, Sariyah's boyfriend, and this is my aunt Lisa."

"Hi honey, Kaysin has told us a lot about you. I am sorry we had to meet under these circumstances."

"It's a pleasure to meet you."

"Family of Kaysin Johns."

We all stood up at once.

"We are Kaysin's family." Sariyah says

"Hi, I'm Dr. Khan. Kaysin is heavily sedated she was complaining about pain during her examination. She was in and out of conscious when we were checking her injuries. She has a fractured jaw and pains in her ribs. I'm sure they aren't broken, but she is in a lot of pain. Only 2 people at a time usually but I see you are all eager to see her. I will take you to her room."

I have never felt this way about any female even with my daughter's moms, I never had to deal with no shit like this. I want to kill this nigga, but I also wanted to just curl up in the bed. I really feel like a bitch but Kaysin has shown me all women ain't the same. Walking to her room, I have to prepare myself to see her so helpless.

"Damn, Sin." I say when I see her with all the IV's and bandages on her.

"OH MY GOD!" Sariyah screams.

Marcellus grabs her before she hits the floor. I can't believe how she is reacting. Shit is bad, but she is out of control. Marcellus and Ms. Lisa hold her up, so she doesn't collapse again.

"Sin, I thought these days were over. I thought I would never see you in another hospital bed." Sariyah cries.

"Riyah, she will be alright, you know Sin is a fighter."

I am completely lost when I hear her say "she thought those days were over."

We sit there in that room all night. The hospital doesn't bother us about visiting hours, so we never left.

"Adonis baby." Kaysin whispers waking me up out of my not so deep sleep.

"Kaysin, how are you, baby?"

"I'm thirsty, really thirsty."

I grab the water and pour her cup.

"When did they get here?"

"About an hour after us."

"Baby, it hurts so bad."

"You have a fractured jaw and bruised ribs."

"Damn, he fucked me up that bad."

"Yea, and Kaysin, as far as I'm concerned, he's dead."

"Baby, it's not serious."

"It is that serious and when you get better, ain't nothing changing."

"Okay baby, these drugs are kicking in and I'm drifting. I love you."

Did she say I love you? That has to be the drugs talking.

Sariyah

Seeing Kaysin in the hospital bed bought back so many memories of the many nights I had to spend next to her. Praying and pleading that God will pull her through that rough time in her life. When Mama Jean passed, Kaysin felt like her whole world was gone. She suffered from chronic depression. She grew so much and is in better spirits. She doesn't deserve this, and I really want to go give Jayceon a piece of my mind. From what I see, Adonis has that handled. They have only been seeing each other a short amount of time but he has been with us in the hospital from the time she walked in. He is showing that he really cares, and I really appreciate that.

Life has been great for both of us, so I don't know why the devil is trying to work against us. After the party and baby shower, my calendar has been booked to capacity. Jillian really helped me with all the publicity she gave me. She blessed me with another bonus for the baby shower. Asia wasn't welcomed because Jillian felt she didn't know how to act in public places and was afraid she would embarrass the brand.

Now I am here sitting in my bed, reminiscing on all the good things that have been going on because if I continue to think about Kaysin's condition, I will for sure lose it.

"Hey babe, how are you feeling?" Marcellus comes out of our bathroom, with a towel wrapped around his waist. Normally, that's all I needed to be all over him but today I just wasn't in the mood.

"I'm here is the best answer I can come up with right now."

"She is going to pull through and be better than ever."

"But when is the question? I need a brunch date right now." We both laugh.

"Kaysin loves her a good mimosa."

"Me too."

"Babe, I want to talk to you about something."

"Let's Talk."

"Aunt Lisa told me my moms popped up at the house again begging to see me." Marcellus says with anger in his voice.

"Do you want to see her?"

"Nah, I'm not ready yet but I know I will be eventually. Will you support me like be with me when I see her?"

"Celly, I'll support through anything and everything you do."

"So, if I told you I wanted to rob a bank."

"Just call me Bonnie."

"That's why I love you."

We cuddle and fall asleep. We are both drained from the day. Marcellus always supported me, so I never had to think about whether I would support him.

3:00am

I wake up sweating and my stomach in knots. I run to the bathroom and throw up all my food from dinner. Marcellus didn't even move in his sleep. I decide to take a shower and head to my office. I have been having trouble sleeping and battling with the fact that I may be pregnant. I thought I wanted to be now that I am having these symptoms, I'm scared shitless. At this time, I usually call Kaysin and tell her how I'm feeling.

"Baby, what are you doing in here?" Marcellus says shaking me out of my sleep.

"I couldn't sleep last night, and I didn't want to disturb you, so I came in here."

"You can never disturb me. You feel okay?"

"Yes, I'm good. I'm gonna get ready to go see Sin."

"She should be up and alert now. Give her my wishes if you are still there when I get off I will come meet you."

"Okay baby." Marcellus gives me a kiss on the forehead and heads out the door.

I get dress and head to CVS. Walking into the pharmacy; I have so much anxiety. As I walk down the aisle to grab what I need, my heart pumps out my chest. I grab 5 pregnancy tests and head to the counter.

"Your total is 60.53."

"I don't need all of these, they all do the same thing,"

"Honestly, you can go to the 99-cent store and get one for a dollar."

"One is good enough" I chuckle as I hand her my card.

I grab the test and make my way to the hospital.

"I'm here to see Kaysin Johns."

"They moved her to the recovery floor." The receptionist said

"Why did they move her!? Is everything okay?"

"Everything is fine. She is getting discharged within the next couple of days."

I head to the recovery floor and finally find Kaysin's room. I'm not surprised to see Adonis sitting there talking to her.

"Hey Sin, I wasn't sure if you would be awake," I said smiling "Hey Adonis."

"I've been up all day and I feel so much better so, come love me."

I run over and give her the tightest hug I feel she could bare.

"Okay, not too tight." Kaysin winces in pain a little.

"I am so sorry, boo."

"Y'all have some time and I'm gonna go check on the shop." Adonis kisses Kaysin and gives me a hug goodbye.

"If you need anything at all, don't hesitate to call me. I will be right back here."

"What am I? Chopped Liver."

"I meant from outside."

"I got her Adonis, she is in good hands."

As soon as Adonis walks out, I waste no more time.

"I couldn't do this without you." I pull the pregnancy test out of my bag.

Kaysin eyes widen.

"Are you pregnant?"

"We are about to find out together. If you weren't in pain, your ass would be coming in the bathroom with me."

I go to the bathroom and pee on the stick. I don't wait for the results. I put the cap on and wipe it down. I hand it to Kaysin and we wait.

She scoots over so I can lay in the bed with her.

"Okay, on the count of 3, I am going to move my hand."

"1…. 2….3" We say in unison.

Kaysin moves her hand

"What does two lines mean?"

"Two lines means my new name is Auntie Sin."

"OMG, I am going to be a mommy." Tears fall from my eyes.

Kaysin

These last 3 days have been such a blur. My body aches, and I can't do anything without somebody helping me. Adonis has been by my side since the beginning. We haven't spoken about the flowers or him asking me to be with him. Every time the doctors come in, he refers to me as his girl and shows major concern.

Sariyah couldn't wait to drop this bomb on me. We are having a baby. Yes, we. That baby is mine just as much as it's hers and Marcellus. We spent all day talking about the baby and Adonis. I can't believe how our lives changed so fast.

"Riyah, you will be an amazing mother. Look how well you take care of Marcellus, your first child."

"Oh hush, that is a grown ass man."

"Who told you that?" I laugh

Dr. Kahn enters my room.

"Kaysin, wonderful news, your x-rays came back and though your ribs are bruised, there isn't internal damage. We are drawing up your discharge papers for you to be released today. The only catch is you must say on bed rest for a week. No straining and lifting heavy things. I will set up a follow up appointment for you before you return to work."

"Thank you so much, you have been great, but I am ready to go home."

"I filled two prescriptions for you, please take them as it reads on the bottle and if you experience any excess pain, please come back without hesitation."

Marcellus shows up in the door and waves, waiting for the doctor to give him the okay to come in. Sariyah gives me a look, which means she doesn't want to tell him about the baby yet.

"Hey Kaysin, looks like you stronger than we all thought." Marcellus chuckles.

"Oh please, you already knew I wasn't going to be in this shit for too long."

"THANK GOD, you can finally go home."

"Sariyah, I've been here for three days and I'm not dying."

"I know, all the bad memories here makes want to get you out of here as soon as possible."

I tried not to relive my past the whole time I've been in this hospital. I spent way too many nights in the hospital on suicide watch and getting my stomach pumped from all the things I tried to consume to end my life. This time is different, and I hate Jayceon for putting me here. This isn't over between him and I, but I am sure I will win this battle just like my last one.

My phone rang, Adonis calling

"You good, baby girl?"

"Yes, the doctor said I can go home today."

"Okay, I am coming back to get you."

"Adonis, you was by my side the last two days, I know you need a break. Sariyah and Marcellus are here, and they will make sure I get home safe."

"I'll be there in fifteen minutes."

Just like that, he hangs up on me.

"Adonis is coming back, isn't he?" Sariyah smirks.

"Yea, he didn't even give me a chance to tell him any different."

Dr. Kahn returns with my discharge papers. Sariyah takes me to the bathroom and helps me get dress. When I see myself in the mirror, I break down and cry. My face and neck are bruised, and you can still see the swelling around my eyes.

"Sin, please don't cry, this isn't your fault."

"Look at me, Riyah. Look what he did." I gently touch my face. Though the pain is gone, I can still see all the fucking bruises

"Look at me, Look at us." She holds my hand and we both stare into the mirror. "Sis, you are beautiful inside and out always. Don't let this break you down."

"I need closure before I can move on from this. I need my revenge."

Jayceon needs to pay for what he did to me. Not just this, but for all the years I dealt with things that were unnecessary. I gave him everything I had, and he tried to strip it away from me. He has no idea that Mama Jean raised a solider, and I wasn't the one to be fucked with.

We walk out of the bathroom. Adonis and Marcellus are talking like they are the best of friends. I don't know how long he's been there, but I don't want him to know I was crying. I wipe my eyes once again and head to get my papers.

"Yo, we have to chill sometime and meet up on better terms." Marcellus says.

"Once baby girl is 100% percent, we can have dinner at my crib." Adonis says smiling.

We say our goodbyes and go our separate ways. Adonis helps me with every step and though I appreciate it, I hate feeling helpless.

"Adonis, I got it." I snatch my hand away and get into the car. The ride is silent, and I realize he is going the opposite way from my house.

"Where are we going?"

Adonis ignores me and turns up the music. In return, I turn it down.

"Where are we going?"

When we pull up to his penthouse, I refuse to get out the car.

"Sin, get out the fucking car."

"Take me home, I don't want to stay here."

"What is your problem, you want to go to your house and do what, think about the shit that went down beat yourself up."

"I want to go home."

"Sin, I'm not arguing with you, just get out the car and go upstairs."

I get out the car and slam the door.

"Don't slam my door." Adonis yells.

When we get upstairs, I sit on the couch with my arms folded.

"Sin, what the fuck is your problem?"

"You don't have to feel sorry for me or take care of me."

"Feel sorry for you, why would I feel sorry for you?"

"Don't be here if you don't want to be."

"Sin, before that nigga violated you, I been here and now because you got a couple of bruises. I am supposed to just say fuck you."

"Adonis, where were you? Where the fuck was you when he was beating my ass and trying to rape me. I called you repeatedly, and you didn't answer."

"I had some shit to handle, Kaysin."

"Shit, that's the best you can come with." I cry. "Tell whatever bitch you were handling. She can have you."

"Whoa, what are you even talking about? What bitch?"

"You always answer my calls and you didn't when I needed you the most."

"First of all, I came as soon as possible, and I should've blown that nigga's head off, but I didn't because I'm always thinking about you and your fucking feelings. Secondly, I was at the shop with my manager discussing how my best friend has been robbing my ass every day because I've been so wrapped up in your ass."

"Wrapped up in my ass, you go to your shop every fucking day while I'm at work so just cause a nigga caught you slipping ain't my fault."

"So, it's like that." Adonis looks at me and walks away. Before I could say anything else, he's walking out the door.

Adonis

Driving to the pharmacy to get Kaysin's prescriptions, I couldn't stop thinking about what she said. I ain't mad at her, all the shit she said is true, but she didn't have to say it like that. She isn't the reason Trey was robbing me. I trusted a nigga who didn't deserve my loyalty. These niggas already dead in my eyes. I stop to get food and head back to the house. Me and Kaysin got a lot to talk about and all this shit is getting unveiled tonight.

"Where did you go?" Kaysin met me at the door as soon as she hears my key in the door.

"I went to get your pills, and to see my other bitch." I say in the most sarcastic tone.

"Don't play with me, Adonis."

"Baby girl, I don't even know why you would think I was with another girl and ignoring your calls."

"I know, I was tripping. I'm sorry about the shit I said before you left."

"Shit was real, but I can't blame you."

"So, Trey has been robbing you."

"Yea, he got about 25 stacks."

"Adonis, how can someone take 25 stacks from you and you not realize it."

"Kaysin, I got some shit to tell you, but you can't go running your mouth and don't leave my ass. If you do, I gotta kill you."

"Well, I can't really go anywhere and watch your damn mouth."

"I own a barber shop and the shit makes good money but as you can see, I live a very lavish life."

"So where are you getting all this extra money from?" She looks at me and her eyes tells me she already knows what I'm about to tell her.

"Coke, Pills, and Weed."

"Have you been locked up?"

"Nah, my operation is tight, and my money is clean. The feds ain't on me."

"We good as long as you keep me out of danger and don't get caught and I really mean that shit."

I pick her up and kiss her. This girl is really an angel sent from heaven, but I also know she been through some shit, she too understanding sometimes.

"Adonis, not so rough baby."

"My bad, you sure you good."

"Yea, you make your money as you please as long as you safe and I'm safe. You lucky you told me now though because if you would've waited any longer, I definitely would have walked."

"We had to build that trust first, that's just how shit goes when you in this business. Speaking of business, Jayceon and Trey gotta go."

"Gotta go?"

"Yea, I'm gonna have them killed."

"Baby, it's not that serious."

"You keep saying that shit, and that's not gonna change my mind. I already made my mind up."

I walk into the kitchen and get our food.

"Okay, if I can't change your mind, I don't have energy to go back and forth."

"Kaysin, I told you a secret I was hiding from you, and now it's your turn."

"What are you talking about?" Kaysin looks at me with concern.

"When you were unconscious at the hospital, Sariyah mentioned something about she thought she wouldn't see you in another hospital bed."

Kaysin's body language changes and she looks at me directly in my eyes.

"When Mama Jean passed, I suffered from chronic depression and tried to kill myself many times. I spent a lot of time in the hospital and under suicide watch."

"Damn, why didn't you tell me?" I can't believe Kaysin dealt with that shit. Many people don't make it out of that.

"A part of my past I don't really want to talk about or relive. So, I try to stay far away from hospitals."

"You good now. I'm here to protect you."

"I know baby, again I am sorry about earlier, I am super emotional."

"We good. I got something for you."
I pulled the Gucci bag from behind the couch.

"I am not taking this, so you can take that shit right back to the store or give it to your hoe." Kaysin laughs.

"Kaysin, as my woman, you will take anything I give you and all the hoes are gone, they wasn't getting shit from me when they was around either."

"Adonis, just because you have money doesn't mean you have to shower me with gifts and try to buy my love."

"This is nothing compared to what I plan to give you."
Kaysin opened the box and saw the belt.

"This is the belt I told you not to buy me that day we went to the mall."

"Yup and I still bought it. It's been sitting in the same spot."

"Thanks baby."

"No need to thank me."

"Baby, I want to pay Jayceon a visit."

"Excuse me?!?" I yell. She had to fuck up this moment by bringing this nigga up.

"I need to get closure."

"Yea, we going to get that closure when that bullet hits his skull."

"No, Adonis. I want him to suffer. After all these years, he has put me through so much shit and I don't want to bring any hurt or anger into our relationship."

"Baby, I see what you have been through and I know you want to see him suffer but, at the same time you will go nowhere near him."

"Adonis, we not about to argue about this, don't say I never to. you what my plans were. I am grown, you can't tell me what I can and can't do."

"Sin, I'm not trying to control you. I am trying to protect you and I need you to allow me to do that. Clearly, you think pepper spray and that knife can save you from every situation, but it didn't save you in the last situation and it probably won't save you from the next."

"So, get me a gun." Kaysin scolds.

I don't care that she has an attitude. Kaysin is a stubborn ass female, and she thinks she can solve every problem alone. Now she is asking for a gun trying to get her own revenge. She is really pissing me off because I know she isn't going to listen, and I have other shit to worry about on top of all her shit. This is exactly why I have been avoiding this relationship shit. It never comes easy.

Marcellus

"Baby, I don't feel good at all." Sariyah has been in the bathroom all morning. I acted like I was sleeping when I heard her throwing up. I know she's pregnant, but she hasn't told me yet.

"You probably don't feel good because you are carrying my seed."

"What are you talking about?"

"Princess, seriously?"

"Marcellus, I probably ate something bad and my stomach just isn't agreeing with me."

"Okay, I thought we was good and you sitting here lying straight in my face about you being pregnant."

"Celly, we are good."

"Sariyah, I was there before the doctor walked in to Kaysin's room. I fell back when he came to the door because I didn't know if I should be in the room when he was telling Kaysin whatever she needed to hear."

Sariyah has a guilty look on her face as I explain to her how I know she is lying.

"Kaysin said you will be an amazing mother because you already take care of me. So now tell me why the fuck you are lying to me about being pregnant."

"I was going to tell you."

"When was you gonna tell me because I just asked you and you lied to my face? So, we lying to each other now and we have had many conversations about."

"Marcellus, are you ready for this because if you aren't, that's okay."

"Sariyah, you sound stupid as hell. I've been showing you I want the same as you and now you are asking me if I'm ready."

"Celly, I'm sorry. My emotions are all over the place. I am happy, but I'm also scared."

"First of all, I am ready, I been ready, now is the best time for us. We aren't married or engaged yet, but shit, that doesn't mean I don't want to spend my life with you. We going to spend a lifetime together so why rush something that won't change."

"You have never said anything like that before."

"I shouldn't have to; my actions show it. I'm taking Aunt Lisa out today, so I'll see you tonight."

"Please don't tell her without me."

"You told Kaysin without me. I'll think about it."

I am pissed off she didn't tell me about the baby and lied when I confronted her about it. This is supposed to be one of the happiest moments of my life and she fucked it up for me. Though I am upset with her, it doesn't change the fact I have a little one on the way. I'm about to be a father.

When Aunt Lisa gets in the car, I want to tell her immediately. It means a lot to Princess to tell her together, so I keep it to myself.

"Hey King" Aunt Lisa hugs and kisses me like I'm a 5-year-old.

"Hey Auntie!"

"You ready to drop a grand or 2."

"Do I really need to spend that much?"

"Yes, my daughter-in-law deserves it."

As soon as we get in the mall, Aunt Lisa doesn't hesitate to go straight to the jewelry store. She has me in there for a good two hours looking for the perfect ring for Sariyah. Finally, after she tries on every ring in the store, we make our choice. It is a 2-carat diamond with diamonds all around the band. The ladies in my life are so bougie and extra. My birthday is in a few weeks and that's when I wanted to pop the question. After the shit that happened today, I might postpone.

"Celly, are you ready for your party?"

"What party?"

"My annual shebang I throw you."

"That's not a party Auntie, that's just us getting drunk and reminiscing on all the great times we spend together."

"That's what I call a party."

"Your old ass."

"Watch your mouth boy." Aunt Lisa slaps the back of my head "Let's go eat"

She waits until we are sitting down and eating to bring up what I been avoiding all day.

"Celly, your mother keeps popping up at the house."

"That is the only reason I haven 't been over there."

"I think you should give her a chance. She is doing so much better than she has been."

"What do you mean than she has been?"

"Celly, this isn't the first time your mother has come around, but it is the first time she is requesting to see you."

"So, you've seen her over the years."

"Celly, that's my sister. I am all she has."

"You had me thinking she disappeared all these years, and you knew where the fuck she was."

"Watch your mouth and tone, we are out in public. She told me to never tell you she came around. She wasn't doing well back then. It was best for you."

"I asked you if you spoke to her or saw her and you would tell me no."

"Celly, it was for your own good."

"And it's for my own good to see her now."

I want to pay the bill and get the fuck out of here. So, everybody is keeping secrets from me like I'm the one doing wrong.

"Marcellus, you are a grown ass man that needs to realize a lot of shit. I hate when you get me to cussing." Aunt Lisa whispers hard.

"What the hell do I need to realize?"

"People make mistakes and forgiveness is a part of living. You don't need to build a relationship with her but the least you can do, is give her a moment of your time."

"I owe her a moment of my time and that bitch owes me 18 years of her time. I am sick of you making it seem like just because you raised me, and shit was straight, I am supposed to forget that you aren't my mother and she is," I yell.

Before I knew it, Aunt Lisa's hand slaps me across the face.

"Pay for this fucking food and meet me at the car." She gets up so quickly and disappears out of the restaurant.

I take about 10 minutes to get our food and pay for the bill. I already know the wrath of an angry black woman was coming straight my way when I get outside. Aunt Lisa is sitting on a bench by the parking lot, she gives me a death stare when I finally her. Once we get in the car, all hell breaks loose.

"Don't you ever in your life disrespect your mother like that again. I didn't raise you to disrespect woman and no matter what you say that woman gave you life. I don't give a damn who raised you even if it was me without her you wouldn't even be here." Aunt Lisa is yelling so loud the people in the parking lot looking all in the car "You got me all out of character, yelling and cussing. Marcellus, you will see your mother and I don't want to hear anything else about this."

The ride back to the house is quiet and when I pull up to the house. She doesn't even say bye. She barely lets me get the car to a complete stop before she opens the door.

"Love you Auntie."

Today is one of those days I want to end. At least I got a ring for Princess that I know she will love. I should make her ass wait longer for this damn proposal since she lying and shit.

When I get back to the house, I really don't want to be bothered. I grab a glass of Hennessy for myself and head to the guest bedroom. I'm not sure if I'm over this whole thing with Sariyah, I ain't in the mood to talk. Aunt Lisa hasn't yelled at me like that since I was a youngin'. The way I feel obviously means nothing to anybody around me and therefore I never explain my feelings to anybody. Call me what you want but I know that me changing my outlook on things would come with consequences that make me suffer.

Lisa

"Was that my baby boy?" My sister standing in front of my building as soon as Marcellus pulls onto the block. He wouldn't recognize her since she changed her hair color and put on a few pounds. I'm so angry with Marcellus, but I also don't want him to think I'm trying to set him up. I jump out the car so fast and run into the building.

"Claudia, that was him."

"Why did he pull off so fast? Did you tell him you saw me standing there?"

"No, him and I had a disagreement."

"Was it about me? you two must never fight unless it's about me."

"Claudia, yes it was about you. He doesn't want to see you and I don't blame him."

"You said you would make it happen for me."

"And I am trying damn, I really am trying."

"So, what is the problem, why doesn't he want to see me?"

"Are you kidding me Claudia, you pop up after all these years asking for him now, what about before?"

"I am his mother."

"Yes, his mother that abandoned and left him at my doorstep 18 years ago."

She is getting on my nerves. Claudia is popping up at my house at least 3 times a week now, in hopes to run into Marcellus. I really want to help her but, at the same time I understand where Marcellus is coming from. I have told her a million times he isn't ready and give him more time, he will come around. She has never been more persistent about anything in her life other than chasing a man.

"Claudia, give him more time when he is ready I will call you."

"Lisa, give me his number, I can call him myself."

"I am tired of repeating myself to you two, when I say something why don't you listen. Like mother, like son."

Claudia smiles when I mention her being Marcellus' mother. Why is she smiling at the obvious? That will never change.

"Claudia, listen. Marcellus is a grown man who makes his own decisions and I can't pressure him to do anything he doesn't want to do. You can't expect him to just welcome you with open arms after you have been gone all these years. You can't take back all the hurt and abandonment he may feel. Just give him some damn time."

"I am trying to change that. I have been trying for the last two months so I am tired of trying to please him. This is why I left."

"No, you left because you didn't want to be a mother anymore. That boy didn't deserve what you did to him. He was and still is an amazing human being."

"I guess I will never find out."

Claudia walked out the door without a second look back. The same way she walked out the door 18 years ago. Thinking back to that day makes me think about how my baby boy really feels and knows seeing his mother isn't best for him right now. Things are going so well for him and I don't want my sister to ruin it with her selfish ways.

18 years ago

"Hey sister, how have you been?" Claudia enters my house with the key I gave her. Even though I told her to only use it when I'm not home. She refuses to knock and always welcomes herself in.

"I'm good, would have been better if you knocked or rang the bell."

"Why do I need to knock or ring the bell if I have a key?"

"That key was given to you for emergency usage only."

"Well, there is an emergency, Marcellus has to use the bathroom."

"That's why he flew pass me without saying a word."
Marcellus comes from the back with a huge smile on his face.

"Sorry Auntie, I had to use the bathroom so bad and mom was rushing me out of the house."

"It's okay baby, now come and give me a big hug and kiss."
He runs over and embraces me like never before. Marcellus loves to
come spend time with me since his mother always has somebody in the
house with them. They barely spend any quality time together. When he
stays with me, we do everything under the sun. He knows I always spoil
him to death.

"Marcellus, make sure you behave for Lisa."

"Girl please, my baby never gives me any issues."

*"Come here baby, you know mama loves you and I will always
love you."*

"I love you too mama."
Claudia is acting super funny today. She never tells Marcellus to
behave, and she hugs him like she will never see him again.

"Celly, go in the living room. Let me talk to Lisa for a minute."

Marcellus runs to the living room, turns the tv on and zooms
into his cartoons like nobody else is around.

"Lisa, I need you to keep Marcellus."

"I know, he is spending the weekend over here."

*"He thinks he is spending the weekend here, but he will live
here."*

*"No, the hell he isn't. You will come get your son on Sunday
like you always do."*

"I got shit to do, and he is always cramping my style."

"Cramping your style, you sound stupid."

*"You always telling me how much you love him and how you
wish you had one of your own, so now here he is."*
I can't believe what my sister is asking me to do. She is telling me she
isn't coming back for her child and she has better things to do. What
kind of bullshit is that?

"When are you coming to get him?"

*"I don't know yet, I need time and I promise I will be back to
get him."*

*"What am I supposed to tell Marcellus when he is ready to go
home."*

*"He may ask for me, but I doubt it. He is better off here,
anyway."*

"Claudia are you serious right now?"

*"Yea, I wasn't going to tell your ass, but I thought I would give
you the courtesy,"*

"Give me the courtesy you have got to be kidding me."

"I packed his bag with more than enough clothes. If I can, I will send money, thanks sis, Joe is downstairs waiting for me. Love you."
She walks to the living room and gives Marcellus another kiss and hug than she disappears.

When Sunday comes, she isn't coming to pick him up and Marcellus doesn't seem to look forward to leaving so I don't even mention it. We follow the same routine for two weeks until one day, on the ride home, Marcellus finally asks me the words I had been dreading.

"She isn't coming back." *Marcellus is sitting in the backseat looking out the window. He said it so low, I can barely hear him, but I know exactly what he said.*

"What you said baby?" I turn down the music.

"My mom isn't coming back. It has been weeks, and she hasn't even called to see if I am okay."

"I got you baby, she will be back soon."

"I don't care if she comes back, I love staying with you. We spend time together and eat dinner as a family every night."
Hearing him say he doesn't care if she comes back broke my heart. You can tell he is missing a lot of love and affection.

I felt like I owed him the world for what his mother put him through. From that day forward, I filled her shoes and did the best I could. I need a few shots of tequila after dealing with them today. I decide to text Marcellus, I was just upset with how he spoke about his mother and how he acted in a public setting. I damn sure didn't raise him that way.

Me–Celly, I love you. I'm not mad that you don't want to see her, it upset me you got out of character and was being disrespectful. Call me tomorrow XOXO.

Sariyah

I can't believe Marcellus knew about my pregnancy this whole time. I was so nervous to tell him. We just got back in a good space in our relationship and I didn't want to make things complicated with a baby. We discussed having a baby frequently, something was just telling me to wait a little longer to tell him. That plan backfired and now Marcellus is giving me the silent treatment.

When he comes back from going out with Aunt Lisa, he walks right pass me and heads to our guest room. I know I need to give him some space because I would be pissed off at myself if I was him too. I was getting ready to call Kaysin to cry about how bad I fucked up, but my phone rings.

Here comes more bullshit.

"Hello." I say dryly.

"Sariyah Jhene, seems like you forgot my number."

"Mom, the phone works both ways, it's been weeks since we spoke to each other."

"Whose fault is that, not mine." My mother yells into the phone. "You always so wrapped up with your man."

"Yes, I am so wrapped in my man and not running my business."

"How is your little business going?"

"My BIG business is doing exceptionally well, actually. I am pretty booked for the next two months."

"Well, look at my beautiful daughter getting her coins and not sharing with her mother."

"Ma, I gave you money not too long ago."

"That little change you gave me, that is long gone. Can you quick pay me 2 grand."

"So, that's all you called me for." I was livid but expected that from her.

"I called you to check on you but you say you booked and busy so that means there is money to spare. With these events, you get deposits and stuff like that."

"I have bills of my own, and a baby on the way."

That last part slips out, but she is pissing me off always calling me for a handout. She needs to stop depending on me to take care of her. She has a job and gets a paycheck every week, so I don't understand why it's my responsibility to pay her rent every month.

"You said you have a baby on the way."

"Yes, mother of mine, I am having a baby."

"Sariyah, your business is taking off and you going to mess it up with a baby."

"I am not messing up anything, this baby was damn near planned."

"So, you planned for a baby at the peak of your career."

"You are clueless. I can work through my whole pregnancy and when I have the baby, I have enough money saved to take a leave. I also have the option of my wonderful man will take care of us if I decided to never work again."

"Marcellus is not making that much money."

"Ma, you don't know what he is making or how things are in my household, you only looking for a handout."

"So, are you going to send it or not?"

"No, I am not. Figure out how you going to pay your own bills."

I hang up and block her number. Sometimes you have to block people even if it's your mother. I quickly dial Kaysin's number.

"I miss you." I cry as soon as Kaysin answers the phone.

"I miss you too," Kaysin says laughing. "You sound terrible."

"Can I come see you?"

"Yes, please do, Adonis has held me hostage. He won't let me go anywhere until I am fully healed. The doctor says I can go in tomorrow and he wants to make sure I don't need to wear the bandages anymore."

"Okay, I am on my way. Do you need anything?"

"No honey, you are enough. I'll text you the address."

I throw my jacket and run to my best friend. When I get to Adonis' building, Kaysin isn't lying when she says his place is beautiful. I haven't even gotten upstairs yet, and I'm already in awe at how beautiful the building is.

"Ms. Kaysin is expecting you. The code for the elevator keypad is 0608. Enjoy your visit Ms. Sariyah." The doorman unexpectedly greets me.

He knows my name and everything. Kaysin lucked up with this one. Adonis seems like a genuine and loving person. I am happy for Sin; she deserves it. I got on the elevator. When the door opens straight into the apartment, I am convinced I'm in another part of town.

"Sariyah baby."

My eyes are popping out of my head with how beautiful this apartment is.

"Kaysin, this is Adonis' apartment. This is beautiful."

"Actually, you would consider this a penthouse. It's been years since I had an apartment." Adonis says grinning "Hey Sariyah, where is Marcellus? I was hoping to see him today."

"He is home, I didn't know you would be here."

"Well, since he isn't, I can leave ya'll to your girl time or whatever. I am tired of babysitting her spoiled ass anyway, I need a break."

"Adonis, don't make me slap you, I don't need a babysitter. You won't let me go anywhere."

"I will not risk losing you or you getting hurt again." Adonis kisses Kaysin. "I'll be back later, baby."

As soon as Adonis disappears into the elevator, I'm going a mile a minute.

"Kaysin, this penthouse is fucking amazing."

"Yes girl, I told you," Kaysin says smiling. "This makes my apartment look like a box."

"Are you happy?"

"Sariyah, I haven't been this happy in years. He caters to my every need and we click. Everything about him screams too good to be true."

"Don't think like that, he is good and true to you."

"I told him I love him when I was in the hospital."

"What did he say?"

"He doesn't know I know I said it. I haven't mentioned it and I was high as a kite."

"Did you mean it?"

"I'm not in love with him but I care about him a lot."

"Just keep everything going slow, you two will be fine." Kaysin is glowing. Her face lit up every time she spoke about him. Under the circumstances that had them stuck with each other for the past week, she has nothing but good things to say about him. So, I am ready to drop all my problems on her.

"Marcellus overheard us in the hospital."

"What?"

"Yes, he confronted me about being pregnant and I lied." I tear up "He then told me, he overheard us talking at the hospital and couldn't believe I was lying to him."

"The real question is why you didn't tell him?"

"Sin, I have no idea, something was just telling me he wasn't ready for the news but sadly I was wrong."

"Well girl, for once I have to side with Marcellus on this one, you fucked up."

"I know, that's why I am giving him space but eventually I will apologize and let him know it won't happen again."

"Please do because that was wrong."

"Guess who called me today to add to my sorrows."

"Santina Clinton." Kaysin always knew the right answers.

"She asked me to quick pay two thousand dollars, and I slipped and told her I'm pregnant."

"That couldn't have been good."

Adonis

Finally, a breath of fresh air. I been hauled up in the house with Kaysin, taking care of her. That nigga Jayceon fucked up her bad. Baby girl couldn't do anything by herself for the first 3 days. I didn't mind being around her; we learned a lot of shit about each other. I didn't let her out of my sight, she couldn't go anywhere without me. I called up some people I know to redecorate her place. Everything brand new because she deserves it. She deals with way too much shit in business and personal life. Kaysin came into my life and changed my views on everything. I never trusted females because all the bitches I knew was looking for a handout. She constantly let me know she didn't care how much money I had or how I made it. She only cares about me and that shit is hard to find.

Things at the shop were good. I got a new safe installed and Trey can't even be seen on the block of the shop, niggas was calling my phone immediately if someone spotted him. That nigga had a bunch of shit coming his way. Pulling up to the shop, shit is looking real shaky, but I had gotten no calls that anything was going on. The gate is open, but the sign on the door says closed. I parked right in front and put my piece on my waist. I'm tired of people fucking with me, as a boss I shouldn't have to come to my place to babysit these motherfuckers. I guess I gotta go back to the way I was, the boss nobody fucked with. I open the door. Nobody is in the shop and the lights were off. I hear the commotion in the basement, and I recognize the voice. This nigga wants to die.

"Yo, what the fuck is the safe code? This nigga gonna switch shit and not even tell me." Trey yells at Shawn.

"Trey, fuck you and your disloyal ass." Shawn is tied up to a chair looking all fucked up.

Trey punches him, and it looks like he was beating his ass for a while. Shawn isn't budging with the safe code.

"You ain't getting in that safe, that shit is mine and only mine." I have to step up before he kills Shawn. I point my gun right at his head.

"Donz, where the fuck you been nigga? This nigga changed the safe code."

"Trey, how stupid do you think I am?"

"Real fucking stupid." Trey laughs. "Nigga, I have been taking shit from you for years."

"Nigga, you were like my fucking brother."

"That's what you thought. Nigga you been spoiled since we were kids got every fucking thing you wanted. You never asked me to be your partner in any of this shit."

"Nigga, I fed you. When I ate, you were eating right beside me."

"Nah, you gave me what you felt was necessary. All this fucking money you got and you crying over a few thousands."

"More like a hundred thousand dollars." I yell. "You fucked up."

Trey pulls his piece out and points it at me.

"So, it's me and you nigga."

"You gonna shoot me."

"You pulled your piece on me first so it's whoever shoot first." Without a second thought, I pulled the trigger and Trey hit the ground.

"You thought I was a soft nigga that wouldn't pull your card. I treated you like family and you shit on me. Now, I ain't heartless like a lot of these niggas so I'm gonna let you live but don't come to my shit again."

I turn around and untie Shawn. As soon as his arm was free, he pushed me out the way. He pulls his piece and shot Trey right in the head.

"Oh shit, you could've warned a nigga."

"By that time, that motherfucker would have killed your ass."

"That nigga was ready to end me, this shit is crazy."

Looking back at Trey, he still has his gun in his hand. Seeing him laid out on the floor fucked me for a second that really was my brother and I love him. But, I guess my grass is way too high because I didn't see this snake.

"Do you need me to take you to the hospital?"

"Nah, nigga I'm good." Shawn winced in pain "He hit like a bitch, anyway."

We laugh, and I go over to the safe and pulled out five thousand.

"Yo, thanks for holding me down." I handed Shawn the money.

"Nah, I don't need that. You know I got my own little stash."

"Man, take this shit."

"Aight nigga, I'm not giving this shit back so don't ask."

"How we gonna clean this shit up."

"I got you boss, just get up out of here." Shawn pulls out his phone. "Go back home to wifey, she good yet?"

"Yea, she holding it together. That's another motherfucker on my list."

"Just say the word."

Shawn was not only my shop manager but my shooter when things got heated. Nobody ever suspects anything with him. He is overqualified for this position but the best at it. He has a master's in accounting and business. We met back in college and I got him out of a lot of shit with our professors. Even though he was smart that nigga hated school and probably wouldn't have gone to any classes if I didn't push him every day. I don't trust many people, but Shawn has proved his loyalty, so he better not pull no Trey shit. I wised up and niggas won't catch me slipping. After I leave the shop, I need a drink. I haven't been this stressed in my life. Shit was running smooth just a few months ago. Now it's getting out of hand and I need to get it into order. I pull up to Charlie's and I'm ready for a few shots of Hennessy. Charlie's is a local spot that everybody in the hood goes to. It has good ass food and strong drinks. This spot is supposed to be an upscale place but, the hood loves it and Charlie ain't turning nobody away.

I pull up a chair at the bar.

"What's good Charlie?" I yell to get his attention "Let me get two shots of Henny."

"Damn, Dons you must have had a rough day." Charlie is always watching my liquor intake and making sure I'm good to drive home. So, when I asked for two shots, he has to be so fucking nosey.

"Rough week, Today I found out my best friend has been robbing me blind right under my nose."

"Who, Trey? I could've told you that. That boy has a problem, remember back in the day when I had him bussing tables. He would steal the waitresses tips and say the guests wasn't leaving any."

"How you found out?"

"I caught his stupid ass on camera."

"I was always there for him and he fucked me over."

"Keep that grass cut, son." He laughs "I haven't seen you in a minute."

"Yea Charlie, I have a lady now she has been keeping me locked up."

"Adonis, you have a lady? I know I am getting old, but I think my hearing is still there."

"She is something different and I am happy, I don't want to be a player no more."

About 6 shots later, I'm still talking about Kaysin. Charlie is all ears.

"Son, it sounds like you in love,"

"Nah, shorty is nice but I ain't in love."

"Dons, time don't mean a damn thing. I feel in love with my wife soon as I laid my eyes on her. May God rest her beautiful soul."

"I definitely feel like she is the one."

I hear somebody laughing in the background.

"Oh, she is the one." Cassie giggles

"Cassie, I don't have time for your shit, I cancelled you a while ago."

"Yea, because you didn't want a relationship, and I was tired of being mistreated." Cassie says as she walks closer.

"Back the fuck up."

I pull my phone out to call Kaysin. I don't need no shit to go down between me and Cassie and Kaysin find out. I don't know how woman find out, but they do.

"Hey baby."

"Sin, I'm sorry baby but I need you to come get me."

"Why you sound like that? Are you drunk?"

"I had a few drinks." I laugh at the concern in her voice

"Babe, who you talking to?" Cassie says loud enough for Kaysin to hear here

"Adonis, who the fuck was that?" Kaysin yells into the phone. "Where the hell are you?"

"Charlie's, down the block from the shop."

Before I could say anything else, Kaysin hangs up on me.

"Yo, what the fuck is your problem?"

"Did I make your little girlfriend upset?" Cassie grabs my hand "Just wait till she gets here."

Cassie sits next to me in the bar. The place is packed, so I can't move anywhere else. I'm too drunk to stand without stumbling or getting dizzy. Not even 15 minutes later, Kaysin and Sariyah come through the door. Kaysin is livid running towards me.

"This is the bitch I heard on the phone." Kaysin screams "So I am at home recovering from this crazy shit and you out here with the next bitch getting drunk."

"Kaysin, chill."

"Yea, Kaysin you need to chill." Cassie taunts Kaysin as I watch to make sure she doesn't kill her.

"Bitch, I am not the one."

"I am the one though." Cassie stands up

"Whoa, shit ain't going down like that. Kaysin, why would I call you if I was out with someone else."

"So, who is this bitch?"

"Someone who screams his name over and over again."

I already know Kaysin isn't with the shit. I don't want her fighting because her ribs are still fucked up.

"Yo, I don't like disrespecting females but Cassie you being a real bitch right now. Sin baby, I came here because some shit went down at the shop and I needed to blow off steam. I used to fuck with Cassie, but I cut her off before we started kicking it heavy."

"You used to fuck with me." Cassie sucks her teeth. "Nigga, that was more than just fucking with each other. You were at my crib almost every night."

"Key word was," Sariyah steps in. "Kaysin, don't give this hoe your time. You need to get your man home."

"Adonis let's go now before I floor this bitch."

I stand up and stumble a little. Kaysin looks at me and shakes her head. She has never seen me this fucked up before.

"Give me your keys."

"Bye baby, I'll see you around," Cassie smiles.

Before I can stop Kaysin, she swings a punch so hard. Sariyah is right, I'm with Mayweather Jr.

"Don't let me see you around, your disrespectful ass."
Kaysin grabs my keys and helps me to the car. I see her give Sariyah a hug and then she gets in the driver's seat and drives us home. As soon as we get upstairs, Kaysin has no remorse for how I'm feeling.

"First of all, why the fuck did you drink that much? Second of all, why was she even that comfortable next to you and trying to disrespect me and third, why is the first time I hear from you, your ass is drunk in a bar with the next bitch talking into your phone."
I really want to answer all her questions but only one answer came out.

"I love you."

Kaysin

I am livid when I hear a female's voice talking in Adonis' phone. All I see is red. So many things go through my mind. Sariyah and I waste no time to get to the destination. If Adonis is cheating on me, I'm about to catch his ass red-handed. When I walk into that restaurant and see her sitting next to him. I instantly go into crazy mode.

I try to keep my cool, but that bitch asks for the haymaker I give her. I'm ready to give Adonis scream his ear off with this shit he pulled. He is about to get all the shit I feel at this moment until he catches me off guard with drunk ass.

"I love you."

I'm speechless and now even more confused with what he said.

"What did you say?"

"Kaysin, I said I love you."

"Don't say shit you don't mean."

"I mean that shit, you don't believe me."

"Not with your drunk ass with another bitch all over you 5 minutes ago."

"It definitely wasn't what it looked like."

"She was all on you and disrespecting the hell out of me."

"Cassie always wants to feel like she is the shit, and nobody can take her off her high horse."

"I'm sure that punch I hit her with knocked her down."

We both laugh, and I smile at him. The eye contact we make with each other is so enticing. I never thought I could feel this feeling so soon. Mama Jean always told me "Love doesn't have a time limit. When you dedicate your time and effort to someone, it will show, and you will feel it."

"I love you too, Adonis."

"I know, you said it when you was doped up on that morphine in the hospital."

"That does not count." I giggle because we both know I'm lying.

"Yeah, Okay." Adonis said "Baby, can you get me some water, I am not feeling too good."

I walk to the kitchen to get Adonis some water. When I come back to give it to him, he is sprawled out on the couch with his mouth wide open snoring. I take all his stuff off, get him a blanket and throw up bucket just in case he needs it. Guess I am sleeping alone, no drunk love making tonight.

I wake up and Adonis isn't in the bed still. When I go to the living room, he is still on the couch laying in the position he was in when I went into the room last night. I have to go to the doctor to get my bandages off and check everything with my body.

"Adonis baby, it's time to get up."

"Damn, what time is it." Adonis says squinting his eyes a vampire trying to block the sun.

"It's 10, my doctor's appointment is at 11. I can go by myself, it's not a big deal."

Adonis pops up so fast.

"Oh no, you not." I can tell he has a hangover.

"Babe, you are clearly hung-over."

"I'll take aspirin and drink some water."

About 30 minutes later, we are both ready to go.

The ride is silent. I'm not sure if it is because his headache or because we both let each other know how we really felt. We arrive at the doctor's office a little early and they immediately take me to the back.

"Hey Kaysin, how are you feeling?" Dr. Khan said

"Actually, I'm feeling 100 percent better. I am ready to go back to work and get my life back."

"Let me check these bruises and make sure you are good to go." After the examination, Dr. Kahn informs me I am all healed up. I may feel pain in my ribs from time to time, but the pain will subside in a few months.

"Thank you so much."

"The pleasure is all mine, Kaysin."

Adonis is looking like a lost puppy sitting in the waiting area for me.

"You ready?"

"Yea, you good shorty?"

"All good, I'm ready to ride your pony."

"Say no more but we have a stop to make."

"What stop is more important than me getting what I've been missing?"

"Slow down tiger, I am pretty sure you will enjoy this."
Though I have a major attitude, I am curious to know where we are going. As I look out the window acting pissed off, I recognize the area. He is finally taking me home. When we pull up to my apartment, I feel like I haven't seen my place in years and sadly, all the memories of what happened come flooding back. Before I can stop the tears, they fall.

"Kaysin, we don't have to go inside if you not ready." Adonis wipes my tears away and kisses my cheek.

"It's now or never, so let's just go in." I let out a deep sigh and get ready to face my fear of reliving that moment over and over.

"Alright, let's go."
Adonis comes around and open my door. He grabs my hand and reassures me I will be fine. My heart is racing, and I feel like I can't live in this apartment anymore. Everything about this place now reminds me of what an asshole Jayceon really is. I open my door and scream.

"Oh my god Adonis, what do you do?!" I scream in excitement. My apartment is completely different. New paint, new furniture, new everything. I am so overwhelmed with emotions and burst into tears.

"Baby girl, you and this crying shit has got to stop." Adonis laugh as I jump on him giving him kisses all over.

"When did you do all of this?"

"I didn't do shit, what nigga you had redecorate? This shit is nice."

"Don't play with me."

"Sin, listen to me, you couldn't live in that space anymore, your place had that nigga written all over it. I know you don't want to move because you worked so hard for this apartment. Plus, it's close to work. So, I bought a new apartment to you." Adonis smiles "Your landlord was being a real bitch, but with a little encouragement, he was good with the changes."

"How much was all of this?" I give him a stern side eye because he knows I don't care about his money.

"That doesn't even matter, and I wouldn't tell you no matter what you do."

I drop to my knees and unbuckle his pants

"Oh really, we will see about that."

Today is the day we make love like never before. All the things he has done for me hasn't gone unnoticed and he knows I appreciate everything. There is nothing like a woman who pleases her man in the bedroom that's the best form of thank you in their eyes.

We both doze off after our lovemaking session in my brand-new California king bed. He has satin sheets on the bed and they feel so damn good on my skin. I pull out my phone and call Sariyah. I should have snuck into the bathroom, but I secretly want him to hear the conversation.

"Hey Sin, I don't have to bail you out, right?" Sariyah laughs

"Girl, that was a big misunderstanding but that little hoe can still catch these hands."

"How you feeling?"

"Honestly, the best I've felt in a really long time."

"I love how you sound, I can feel that smile through the phone but why the hell you so happy?"

"Adonis renovated my whole apartment and erased every memory of that fuckboy in this place. Bitch, it's not as bomb as his big ass place but this shit is mine and it's beautiful."

I peek over at Adonis who is clearly eavesdropping and pretending to sleep. I can see him smirking. Right where I want him if only he knew.

"Oh, I gotta see this shit. Answer my FaceTime."

Sariyah waste no time to FaceTime me. As I give her a tour of the house, her mouth drops open.

"Sin, that's your place?" I go to the window, so she can see that the outside looks exactly the same.

"Yes baby, this is all me."

"Shit, you got a keeper, finally." Sariyah surely emphasized that finally.

"I know girl, I waited too long for this." I can't believe this is my life right now. After all the shit I've been through, finally the Lord has answered my prayers. "Enough about me, how are you feeling?"

"I can't keep anything down. This baby is kicking my ass already."

"Are you and Marcellus good now?"

"We haven't really spoken about anything, but he has been attentive making sure I am good."

"He will be over that in no time. Y'all come over here for game night tonight."

"Okay, we will be there at 8."

"Love you."

"I love you too,"

Marcellus

This nigga Adonis has me feeling like I need to step my game up. I know that Sariyah is good and happy. But damn, this nigga gave Kaysin a whole new apartment in her old apartment. I am still trying to feel him out, but he seems like an okay dude. I don't keep too many niggas close for more reasons than one. It's too many snake ass niggas either hating on you, trying to kill you or steal from you.

"Yea, I own a barbershop, it's a family heirloom but I'm turning that shit into a real moneymaker."

"Nigga, I ain't checking your pockets or nothing. But Sariyah told me about your penthouse and you remodeled this whole place in about 2 weeks. So that shit making money like that."

"You gotta work the system bro. I have a few investments under my belt too and I can definitely put you on."

"I mean I make good money now, but more money won't hurt."

"What you doing on a day to day."

"I'm a bank manager at Downtown Federal. I'm looking at some new money, so I'll be making 6 figures soon."

"Oh, I don't fuck with banks and shit, but I might need to because keeping my money in safes ain't been working out in my favor."

"Why you say that? Safes are secure."

"Yea, but niggas' loyalty isn't. My right hand well so I thought was stealing money from me."

"Guess he had the safe code so, it was easy money."

"Yea bro, and that easy money can easily get somebody hurt."

"Well, listen come down to the bank tomorrow, I'll set you up."

"Thanks for looking out."

"Looks like you a part of the family now, so I gotta make sure you straight."

If Adonis is gonna be with Kaysin, I have to keep that nigga out of trouble and away from the bitches. He gave off the same vibes I have about snakes but that's because his man was stealing from him and he didn't even know it. That's fucked up. I should of ask him how much but that's honestly none of my business.

"Y'all ready to get y'all asses whipped for this first couples game night."

"Marcellus, let Adonis know he don't want this."

"Listen man, these ladies take this shit seriously you and Kaysin will not speak for days so be on your A game."

"I ain't got nothing to worry about me and baby girl got this."

After hours of us drinking and playing games, it is time to call it a night. Sariyah is getting agitated and I know she is ready to go home. Kaysin ain't gonna kick us out, so I have to cut the night.

"Aight guys, this is the last round."

"You guys can stay in the guest room if you like." Kaysin is tipsy and isn't ready for us to leave.

"Sin, when the hell did you get a guest room."

"About a week ago." Adonis mocks Bobby Shmurda.

"Y'all are both drunk." Sariyah says laughing at them "Sin, I'm tired."

"My baby is wearing you out."

"Baby?!" Adonis yells. "No wonder you didn't take a sip all night."

"Kaysin, you didn't tell him."

"Nah girl, that was y'all business to tell."

"Well, let's call it a night, hopefully you won't be the only one pregnant Sariyah."

We all look at each other and laugh. This nigga is clearly drunk or is he serious? As soon as we get out the door, Princess is acting funny.

"Gimme the keys, Celly,"

"I'm good to drive, babe."

"Gimme the fucking keys."

I'm not about to argue with her about driving home. Sariyah never wants to drive so I need to take this opportunity.

"You had a good time."

She keeps her eyes on the road and doesn't say a word. She acting like she doesn't even hear me.

"Sariyah, did you have a good time?"

Once again, she ignores me. I don't know what the fuck her problem is, but I don't have the energy to go back and forth with her moody ass. When we get out the car, she walks off fast and I run to catch up to her. If I didn't, she would've locked my ass out.

"What the fuck is your problem? You were just fine at the house."

"Foyer."

"What?"

"The fucking word was foyer."

"You can't be serious right now."

"I am serious as a fucking heart attack, you let that rookie ass couple beat us."

"Kaysin isn't a rookie to Taboo though, and that damn Adonis seems like a natural. We lost by like 5 points."

"You lucky I want a foot rub, or your ass would be in that guest room." Sariyah says sarcastically.

I have to deal with this shit for the next 9 months. Lord, please pray for me. I rub Sariyah feet until she falls asleep and take my ass to bed. I don't know what the hell to do with her ass.

I told Adonis to be at the bank when we open. So, he can be my first client. I don't mind being his personal banker because that nigga needs it. My degree in accounting might have me quit this damn job and work for him personally. I don't think he can afford my 6-figure salary, but a nigga can be curious.

Walking into the bank, everybody is already there. My team is tight, and we support each other.

"Good morning, hope y'all enjoyed your weekend."

"I did and how was yours?" Corrine follows me into my office.

She has a low-cut blouse and a pencil skirt that really shows off her body. Corrine is fine as hell but nothing she does can make me stray away from my shorty.

"It was good, just announced to my family Sariyah and I are expecting." Thought maybe if I told her I had a baby on the way her thirsty ass would go away.

I go to sit down, and she leans over my desk with her titties all on display. I am in a compromising position right now.

"Congratulations Daddy."

Adonis walks in and gives me a side eye.

"Sorry to interrupt whatever this is."

"No interruption at all, thank god you came in." I dap Adonis "Corrine, you can see yourself out."

"No introduction." Corrine stares at Adonis from head to toe.

"Nah shorty, no introduction needed." Adonis firmly says as he takes a seat.

Corrine looks hurt and walks out the office.

"Man listen, I don't know what the fuck is going on, but that didn't look too good."

"Nah bro, it's not even what it looks like."

"Shorty is bad as fuck."

"I know, and she won't leave me the hell alone."

"She knows about Riy."

"Yes, and Princess knows about her thirsty ass too. It's taking me too much strength to keep Sariyah from coming down here."

"I've encountered them when I was in a comprising position, and it ain't pretty."

"I've been with Princess for 5 years, you don't know half the stuff her and Kaysin have done."

We both laugh. We have crazy ass females.

"Alright, how does this shit work?"

"You have never had a bank account before."

"I have access to one account, but I didn't set that up, my pops did. My manager at the shop handles all the bank shit."

"Well, just fill out this paperwork." I hand Adonis the bank application "How much you got today."

"75 stacks."

"Get the fuck outta here." Adonis opened his duffle bag and there is damn sure 75000 in there.

"I told you I have a few investments and I keep ALL my money from them."

"Bro, you made all this from your barber shop."
I already know this nigga is lying. Before I put this money in the bank, I want to make sure he isn't tryna put me in a fucked up position.

"Nah nigga, most of it is from my second business, the one I own under the table. The shop money is in a business account."

"So, you be in the gym heavy, pushing weights."
Adonis already knows what I'm getting at. I'm not tryna put that shit out there at my place of business. I wonder if Kaysin knew this nigga was lacing her off of his dirty money. Knowing her crazy ass, she probably does. She didn't tell Sariyah yet because Princess can't hold anybody secrets; she tells me everything.

"Yea, I'm pushing major weights, will that interfere with this right now." Adonis seems a little concerned yet humored at our lingo.

"Nah not at all, but we gotta meet a few times."

"Aight, 25,000 can go in the account today and I'll come back and put the rest in at the end of the week."

"Yea & imma set you up with a few cards, we about to make this money legit.

Adonis

Marcellus is a nigga I need on my team somehow. He needs to quit this wack ass bank job and fuck with me full time. He knew a lot of shit about money. I know I ain't swiping no damn cards, so I'm gonna give that shit to Kaysin & she could swipe away. That day I took her to the mall was the first time I used my damn card in years. I didn't want her wondering why I carried that much money on me. I have been using cash since I was a lil' nigga. My pops would give me 500 dollars a month. I had to make that shit stretch. Trey was right, I've been spoiled my whole life. My parents did well for themselves and I reaped all the benefits. My moms and pops moved out the city about 5 years ago, we barely even speak now. My pops don't approve of my lifestyle and hate I use his barbershop as a coverup for the drug game I'm into. My moms just back my father up because she feels that is what she is supposed to do. Now I make sure my daughter has the same life I had despite what me and her moms have been going through.

When I get in the car, my phone rings.

"Ma, I was just thinking about you."

"Donny baby, how you been?" My mom cries into the phone. "We haven't spoken in months."

"I'm good ma, just maintaining and I would call more often if pops wasn't acting so stupid all the time."

"Watch yo mouth boy."

"Ma, I'm good and I always will be good, thanks for asking."

"Baby, your dad is sick, and I would love for you to come see him soon and hash out your differences."

"Aight, ma. I'll clear my schedule. I'm gonna bring my girl with me."

"You have a lady!?, oh my Donny baby." My mom screams.

"Yea ma, she is good in my book, so I want ya'll to meet her."

"We will come down next week. Love you ma. I gotta go."

"Next week Donny, keep your promise & make sure you bring my granddaughter with you."

Damn, I told my mom I was bringing Kaysin with me without a second thought and now she is asking for her grandbaby too. What the hell did I get myself into. I don't mind Kaysin meeting Anais, it's her mother I don't feel like dealing with.

Pulling up to Kaysin's crib, I have a lot to tell her and I hope she is ready.

"Baby, how was your meeting with Marcellus." Kaysin greets me at the door with just her bra and panties.

"It went well and you really tryna have a baby walking around her with your skin all out."

"Oh hush, no babies yet."

"Soon though, but come sit down, I have to talk to you about something."

"What bitch do I have to drag now, every time you leave the house?"

"Yo, you always ready to fight."

"Anywhere and EVERYWHERE," Kaysin smacks me with a pillow.

"Since my baby moms, I haven't been with a woman this long without fucking someone else or thinking about telling her I wasn't ready to be exclusive."

"Oh, really I_" Kaysin tries to say something.

"Let me finish before you say anything."

"I am not a man of many words, so take this shit and keep it. As I was saying, you are bomb as fuck and I love you."

"I love you too."

"So next week, we gonna take a trip and meet my family, just got news my pops is sick and we gotta fly out there."

"Whoa, meeting the family, you ready for that."

"As ready as I will be, oh and we going to pick up my daughter in a few days."

"Adonis, you know this means you are stuck."

"Like glue, now go take the little clothes you have on and get to the bedroom."

Kaysin runs to the bedroom so fast and I am right behind her. It never fails, she takes over my body like no other woman ever has. This girl is the one. As usual, she knocks me the fuck out and I wake up to the aroma of food. This feelings shit hit me fast and I don't know what the fuck is going on. Walking out of Kaysin's room, I glance at her from a far and damn I am a lucky man. I know shit is good now and once Kaysin meets Sky and Anais, it might hit the fan.

"Baby, dinner is almost ready."

"Aight, you definitely made me work up an appetite."

"What is she like?"

"Who is she?"

"Your daughter's mother."

"She is cool I guess, honestly don't know what the hell she is gonna say when I pull up with you, but I really don't give a fuck either."

"Adonis, you know I don't like disrespect, I don't want to punch her in her mouth."

"You won't need to, we been over so she ain't checking for me."

"I warned you."

Kaysin's phone rings.

"Sariyah baby, what's wrong?" Kaysin says.

Sariyah

What a shit show this meeting with my mother is. I realize we can never make amends and genuinely love each other.

When my mother arrives, I can already tell she is going to give me her ass to kiss. Though my mother has her fucked up ways, she gave me life and I will always love her unconditionally, but she didn't love me the same. She walks into the restaurant, with a one piece jumpsuit with Gucci shades and Gucci heels. She always lived above her means. She can barely pay her rent but wants to buy designer everything.

"Sariyah Jhene, you are glowing."

"Thanks ma, how you been?"

"I've been good, rent is due next week." She leans her shades down. "Want to help your mother out?"

"We will see ma, my rent needs to be paid also."

"Oh, doesn't your man pay your rent for you? that's what you said on the phone."

"No, I said if I didn't want to pay rent, I didn't have to. You heard what you wanted to hear."

The waiter approaches us and takes our drink order.

"Please bring me a shot of Hennessy and a glass of red wine." Santina asks the waiter. "I will clearly need to it."

"Ma, what is your problem?"

"Problem, oh I have a problem or is it you with the problem."

"I have a few problems like how you can't pay your rent or how you think Gucci and Prada is more important than your lights being on."

"Sariyah, don't you dare try to talk about me and my choices when you are pregnant by a man who hasn't married you after you've given him five long years."

"I am not rushing to get married because eventually it will happen."

"And how the hell are you so sure of that?"

"I'm sure ma."

The waiter returns with our drinks. My mother wastes no time to down her shot of Hennessy and sips her wine. We order our food and the waiter disappears again.

"Yea right, you going to be a baby mama just like most of these other black women in the world."

"You got to be fucking kidding me. Just because you can't keep a man doesn't mean every black woman can't."

"But you damn sure won't be able too, with your independent, I can do it all by myself attitude."

"I've been with mine for 5 years and we aren't perfect, but he damn sure loves me."

My mother always makes me feel like no matter what I do or how successful I am, she will never understand the daughter she raised. The pain I feel sitting at this table with her is indescribable and I want to leave.

"Yea whatever, I thought your father loved me & he left me."

"He left you because you didn't love him, you loved his money and when he died, you were more upset since he didn't leave your ass a dime."

"I loved him, and he selfishly walked out the door."

"Cut the bullshit ma, Daddy was sick, and you did nothing to help him recover and when he died, you hated the fact he left me the little he had left. That's why you didn't help me through college or after that."

"You didn't deserve that money Sariyah, you spent it so quickly and carelessly."

"Carelessly! I spent it on my education and getting my shit together to leave your hellhole of a house and I also paid off all of dad's debt he accumulated in my name because your bougie ass can't live without the finer things in life."

"Sariyah, you still make all that money and can't help your mother out."

"I help you out every fucking month with no questions but now I am done, you don't give a fuck about anybody but yourself." I scream as tears invade my eyes. "My family and I want nothing to do with you, you will never see my child."

The whole restaurant is staring at us. She makes me get out of character and embarrass myself. I run out of the restaurant and pull my phone out. I can't get the words out.

"Sariyah baby, what's wrong?"

"I need you, meet me at my house, please."

After getting into my car, I cry and scream out for my father. I keep so much inside because I am always the voice of reason. My father was always the voice of reason in my life. He was everything and more in my life. His relationship with my mother turned him into a different person. They would argue so much because she felt like he wasn't giving her everything she wanted and needed. When he left her, it was already too late. My father was drinking every day and gambling all his money away. One night after he lost 25,000 dollars, he drank way too much and drove into a pole two blocks away from his apartment and died instantly. That night I lost a huge part of happiness and no one will ever know how I feel. I never let it show because my father wouldn't want me to. His death caused me a lot of pain.

When I pull up to my building, Kaysin is already there.

She meets me at my car and instantly I cry again. This damn baby has me weak as hell.

"What's going on?"

"I had lunch with my mother and it went terrible."

We get to my door, I collapse.

Waking up in the hospital, I have an IV in my arm and I vaguely remember how I got here.

"Finally, you scared the shit outta me." Kaysin runs to my side.

"Sariyah, what the fuck happened today?" Marcellus asks sternly.

"I met with my mom and things didn't go as planned. I was feeling light-headed, but I thought it would pass."

Dr. Khan walked into my room.

"Oh, the gang is here again, y'all love the ER huh?

"Dr. Khan, you got jokes." Kaysin laughs

"Glad to see you doing better Ms. Johns. Now for you Ms. Clinton."

"You know you have a little one on the way, so you must take it easy. You collapsed today due to dehydration and stress."

"That fucking bitch."

"Marcellus, don't do that."

"She is the reason you are in here!"

"Riyah baby, I love you. I am going to head home just wanted to make sure you were good."

"You can leave in a few hours, once we get you filled up with fluids and your heart rate down."

Kaysin and Dr. Khan head out of the door which just left me and Marcellus.

"Don't call my mother a bitch."

"Honestly you wouldn't be here if you didn't meet with her." Marcellus is furious "Did you accomplish anything?"

"I accomplished feeling like a complete idiot and now I know my mom is a money hungry individual who doesn't deserve my love or anything else I have to give."

"You are going to be everything she isn't and more, don't worry baby."

About 3 hours later, they release me from the hospital. They ask me if I want to see the baby and I opted against it. My emotions were all over the place and if I saw mini me, I know I would have been overwhelmed with emotions. I am mentally preparing myself for Wednesday.

Kaysin

All this is too much for one day. Lately I have been feeling like I can't catch a break. I know things between Marcellus and Sariyah were about to get heated so that was my cue to head back home. I left Adonis so abruptly and he also dropped bombs on me. I guess he really is taking us seriously since I am meeting the family and his daughter. I have a few more questions to ask him.

Look who it is calling me.

"Yes, baby."

"Where the hell you at, you said you was coming right back."

"Adonis, I just left the hospital."

"What happened?" The concern in his voice was such a turn on.

"Sariyah collapsed when we got to her apartment and I took her to the hospital."

"Why you didn't call me?"

"Adonis, when was I going to call you? I damn near died trying to keep myself calm."

"I understand, shorty. Well, I am waiting for you, I want to take you shopping and pick up stuff for Anais to take with us."

"You serious about me going with you."

"Yea, what the fuck is the problem, do you not want to go?"

"I would love to go, I remember you telling me you won't take another female to meet your moms unless you plan to marry them."

"Well, if you keep acting right, you might be my wife."

"Oh really, talking like that you might be a daddy."

The relationship Adonis and I have consists of us joking with each other and enjoying each other's company. We didn't force each other into a commitment. It happened. His little hoes pop up more than I appreciate but he handles them before I have to.

When I pull up to my apartment, I told Adonis to come downstairs, so we could hit the mall. I need to get clothes for work tomorrow. Ugh, I don't want to go back to work; I enjoyed this time off.

"Damn, you looking a little stressed."

"Oh no, let me go upstairs and put makeup on."

"Yea, do that." Adonis laughs

I get out the car.

"Baby girl, I'm playing."

"Don't play like that, you are looking at me like you're serious."

I know we about to be fighting at the mall because Adonis always wants to pay for everything and I ain't that female. I can take care of myself.

First stop was Saks. If we went into a store, he could shop to and I can pay for my shit myself.

"Before we go in there, give me your wallet."

"Why the hell do you need my wallet for?"

"You not spending no money today. Adonis puts his hand out. "If you wanted to spend your own money, you should've come alone."

"Well, I'm not giving you my wallet."

"Oh, so this is ya new nigga."

I didn't have time for the bullshit, but I can recognize that ratchet ass voice anywhere.

"Asia, leave me the fuck alone."

"No bitch, I owe you an ass whipping, and my nigga owe you an ass whipping too."

"Who the fuck is this and who is her nigga?"

"Jayceon, motherfucker."

Adonis let out a laugh that even scares me a little. Every time he hears Jayceon name a whole other person comes out of him.

"Please tell that motherfucker to come see me. He knows where Kaysin crib is at and that's where I will be."

Asia never learns and when she attempts to lunge at me. I am ready to give her yet another ass whipping. Why do these bitches always want to try me as a person? I'm really a sweetheart.

Before I could get into a stance, Adonis jumps in front of me.

"Shorty, you don't want this problem for real." Adonis touches his waist and grabs my hand.

"Babe, I had her for real."

"Yea, and the cops would've had you, the way you would've whipped her out." Adonis said. "Now give me your wallet and take this card."

I was going to continue to fight but this battle I know I ain't going to win. I give in and let him take me on a little shopping spree. All the things I would never buy myself I bought. I walk out of the Gucci store like I'm the richest woman in the world. On second thought, I can get used to this.

"You really feeling yourself now." Adonis smiles as I try on my Giuseppe's.

"I always wanted a pair of these but didn't want to spend unnecessary money."

"Well, buy 2 pair and I won't ever ask you to buy another Giuseppe in your life."

"Please Adonis, you spend money like it's nothing."

"I worked hard as a little nigga, now I reap the benefits of being a young boss."

"I want to say that, I'm still working my 9-5."

"So, quit."

"Adonis, no matter how much money you have, I will never quit my job."

"Eventually, you will change your mind and I don't mind taking care of your fine ass."

"So, that's why you want to take care of me because I'm fine."

"Kaysin, you are a trip." Adonis laughs "I would take care of you because you are my woman and I love you. A woman that knows her own heart, how could I not love you." Adonis smiles as he looks at some shoes for himself.

We shop until we drop. Things are about to be hectic between us traveling and trying to prepare ourselves for these meetings that are about to occur. Spending this time together was vital. Meeting the family is a big step, I wish I had a family for him to meet.

I wake up Monday morning, crying inside. Deep down, I want to take Adonis up on his offer and let him take care of me, so I can quit my job. Mama Jean always told me "you can't be a lazy heffah, no matter what a man says, they love a woman with ambition and drive." So, although I felt one way, my ass was getting up and ready for work. I have to show out for my return to work. So, I pull out my Giuseppe's and my Burberry trench. I like the finer things in life, can't say I can afford them without Adonis, so I am in love with my gifts.

"Look who showed up to work today," Kyle says.
I am feeling refreshed and tired of holding my tongue.

"Kyle listen and listen to me good. You are a sexist pig who feel like a woman can't make rank because we look sexy in a dress. I am tired of you targeting me because you know I am steps away from taking your job from right under your nose."

"Ms. Johns, that's no way to talk to your boss."

"Boss, I help you keep this company above water and I'm pretty sure while I was gone, there were many errors made that I will need to correct."

"I don't need your shit today, Ms. Johns."

"That's no way to talk to your employee, don't make me call HR on your behind."
I walk away holding my head high. As soon as I get in my office, Maya runs in behind me and closes the door.

"Kaysin, oh my goodness, I missed you. Kyle has no idea how to run this business without you."
Hearing her say those words makes me smile. I know eventually he would dig his own grave and I won't mind being there to bury him.

"I tried to keep up with all his mistakes and corrected them accordingly but I'm pretty sure I missed a few things. He also hired 2 new general managers for the upstate stores."

"We will need to take a day trip to visit those stores, I can't believe he hired new employees without me."

"He talked so much shit while you were gone and quite frankly I am sick of his ass. We need to impeach his ass."

"Give me a few weeks, let me get a handle on my personal life before I take on his position."
It feels so good to be back at work even with Kyle's stupid ass and his smart-ass remarks. Myah clearly missed me, I don't have to ask for a thing, she is 3 steps ahead of the game.

Jayceon

I've been laying low lately. Shit got out of hand with Kaysin and I snapped. I know her new nigga wants my head. I really don't give a fuck. Kaysin switched up on a nigga and that bitch acting brand new. I have been riding by her job the last couple of days and she is a no show. I wondered if she even still worked there. Finally, I spot her car in her parking spot, so I know she is back at work. I'm sitting in front of her job waiting for her to come outside so I can apologize to her and tell her I didn't mean that shit. She knows I have a temper and I know she not gonna run to her little boyfriend because she all independent and shit.

When we make eye contact, she stays in one place with the look of fear all over her face.

"Jayceon, leave me the fuck alone, you are really fucking crazy."

"Sin, I'm sorry about that shit that went down at your crib, I never meant to hurt you."

"Are you fucking kidding me? You fractured my ribs, busted my lip and gave me a black eye." Kaysin screams "You are fucking dead to me."

"Kaysin, get in the fucking car now." Adonis pulls up and jumps out of his car.

"Hell no, Adonis, if you gonna do something to him, I want to watch. Matter of fact."

Before I knew it, Kaysin punch me in the face. That shit felt like her nigga hit me. Before I know it, Adonis is raining blows all over my body. I get hits in, but this nigga is like the Incredible Hulk. The first time we fought that nigga wasn't this nice. Damn, he must really fuck with her to be whipping my ass like this.

"You don't learn your fucking lesson. Your time is ending sooner than I excepted it to."
He fucked me up but not to a point where I couldn't get to my car and drive the fuck off. I never felt like I needed to kill anybody, but this nigga Adonis had to go. When I pull up to the crib, I sit in my car for a minute. Kaysin fucked up my life in a matter of months. I can't do shit without thinking about her and every bitch I was in that never amounted to anything she is capable of.
A tap on my window breaks my train of thought. I roll the window down and all I see is the barrel of a gun.

"A woman should be loved and cherished, not taken advantage of. Your time just ran out."

That's the last thing I heard before I felt all those bullets pierce my body.

Adonis

Kaysin doesn't know I'm pulling up to her job. It's her first day back and for some odd reason, my gut is telling me I need to go pick her up. As soon as I pull up, I peep Jayceon talking to her. How I knew this nigga was gonna resurface? This nigga is really stupid. Once again, I spare his life because baby girl is right there, and we are right in front of her job. This nigga is a bold ass pussy, he only pops up in public places.

After I whip his ass, Kaysin and I get in my car and speed the fuck off. We don't want to be there if anybody comes out of the building and sees that nigga on the floor. I pull over a few blocks away.

"Yo Shawn, I got a job for you."

"What's good, boss?"

"Member that address I gave you a few days ago, today that shit is in full affect. Look out for a black Toyota with 765 as the last three. Hit me when you done."

"No problem, I got a message for that nigga myself."

"He should be there any minute, so move now."

I look over at Kaysin in the passenger seat, I can tell baby girl is still shaken up even though she acts fearless when he confronted her.

"Thank you." She manages to get out through her fighting back tears.

"No need to thank me, baby. Yo, let's leave today."

"I just got back to work, how am I going to up and leave again?"

"Easy, call your boss and tell him someone confronted you outside of the office and you don't feel safe. They got security cameras and shit, so he will know you not lying."

"You know Kyle fucking hates me and probably going to say some foul shit."

"So, you telling me, I need to get your boss clipped too."

"No babe, I'll contact the CEO and let him know what's been going on. He will have more remorse."

"Aight, pack some shit and I'll come scoop you, I have to go to my crib and get a few things before we head out."
"Okay baby."

Kaysin gets out the car and I watch her fine ass walk to the building before pulling off. That woman is really everything I want and the best thing about it is she ain't perfect at all. She got more shit going on than I ever had to deal with but, I'll be here to pick up the pieces every time. Now I have to call Sky and tell her I am picking up Anais early. Don't think I will mention Kaysin coming until I'm too close to turn around.

"What you want, Dons?" Sky always answers her phone with an attitude for no reason.

"Yo, there is a change of plans. Imma scoop Anais either tonight or early tomorrow morning."

"No, Adonis. You said Friday. She can't miss school for no reason."

"What the fuck you mean for no reason, my father is sick, and we don't know how long he got." I have to exaggerate the truth a little to get her change her mind.

"Damn, I didn't know, you said you were taking her to see your parents."

"Yea, it's fucked up."

"Y'all still not speaking to each other."

"Nah, my moms called and told me, that motherfucker wouldn't have said shit."

Sky knows my history with my family and how shit went down when I first told them I was pushing weight and using the shop as a coverup. Things were real ugly back then. My pops would call my ass and curse me out every day. After a while, the calls just stopped, and I didn't hear shit from him. He ignored all my calls and refused to talk when my moms would call me. Eventually her calls slowed up too, but I know he has something to do with it.

"Aight, I'll pack her a few things, but I already know you will take her shopping."

"You don't even have to pack her clothes, I picked up outfits already. Just her essentials I always forget."

"Essentials?" Sky laughs

"I'm a college graduate, don't fuck with me."

"Aight, see you later."

At least we getting along now because I know she will not take meeting Kaysin very well and she knows I'm heading to see my parents. Sky is the only female that met my parents so now Sky might get in her feelings about how serious Kaysin is in my life.

Shawn: Done

One problem solved. A shitload more to handle.

Marcellus

I haven't been this anxious about anything in a long time. I can't help but smile as I watch Aunt Lisa and Sariyah interact with each other.

"Sariyah Clinton," the nurse calls out.

I hop up so fast and run for the door.

"Boy, would you calm down?" Aunt Lisa laughs.

"Celly, just relax."

It seems like forever for the doctor to finally come into the room and start the sonogram. When she put gel on this object that looked like a huge dick, I had to stop her.

"Whoa doc, what you about to do with that."

"We are about to check your little one out, it's harmless." The doctor says. "Alright Sariyah, you may feel a little pressure."

"You told me it's harmless." This doc had me fucked up.

"Marcellus, if you don't sit your ass down." Aunt Lisa sternly says.

The room got so quiet as the doctor starts the procedure. We are all in awe and just eager to see this baby. Suddenly, a little deformed looking thing popped up.

"Oh shit, that's the baby." I say, smiling so hard.

"Celly, get my phone and FaceTime Sin for me."

This girl couldn't do anything without updating Kaysin.

"It's about time." Kaysin always answers on the first ring. "Oh my god, there is a baby in your belly."

"This baby has a strong heartbeat and from the looks of the growth, you are 12 weeks already."

"I really didn't know, I have been so busy."

"Bitch, you been pregnant for 3 months." Kaysin yells.

We all look at Sariyah waiting for an answer.

"I'm still in disbelief." Aunt Lisa says through her tears.

"This is so beautiful." Kaysin tears up on the damn phone.

"Y'all need to stop with this crying, y'all know I cry every minute." Sariyah says grabbing a tissue.

"Oh, hell no, please tell me it's a boy."

"It's too early to tell, but I see you have a handful." She laughs.

"I'm hanging up, love you guys."

"You will see the doctor again before you come back for another sonogram to find out the sex."

Shit is real. I'm about to be a father. I want to be the parent unlike either one of my parents. My child will never have to wonder if I love them or not. They won't have to wonder when they will have their next meal or if they can get a pair of sneakers. Being a parent isn't easy but I'm sure it's the best thing I will experience. Shit, a nigga already feeling soft.

"Celly, you can drop me with Aunt Lisa, I'll be home a little later."

"Nah, what are you two hiding?" I hit them with the side eye. "Only time you send me home is when y'all are being sneaky."

"If you must know, we are planning out the details of the gender reveal party."

"Do y'all want water?"

"No, why?" They said in unison.

"Y'all being real thirsty." I couldn't help but laugh at my joke.

"Shut up, that's why you aren't invited," Aunt Lisa says.

"I hate planning, that's why I am with a professional. She can do that shit with her eyes closed."

"Thanks baby." Sariyah kisses me and hops out of the car.

"I'm so proud of you King." Aunt Lisa hugs me, almost cutting off my damn circulation.

As usual, I watch them get into the building and speed off. All I'm going to do is cook dinner for Sariyah greedy ass and get me a nap.

Sariyah

As soon as we get in the building, a woman approaches Aunt Lisa and the look on her face shows it's someone she doesn't want to see.

"Claudia, not right now." Aunt Lisa says

Claudia is Marcellus mom's name. I look her up and down and Marcellus looks just like her. This is my opportunity to say something. She is right there and even though I know Aunt Lisa wants me to keep walking. I refuse.

"Your name is Claudia?" I question her.

"Yes, and who the hell are you?"

"Nobody you need to know or be talking to right now." Aunt Lisa stands in between us and pushes me towards the elevator.

"I'm Marcellus' girlfriend, Sariyah."

"Oh, my goodness, how are you, darling?" She leans in to hug me, but I don't have it in me to hug her back

"I'm good, I guess."

"Sariyah, let's go." Aunt Lisa pulls me towards the elevator door.

"Can you and I talk?" Claudia asks with a sincere look in her eyes.

Honestly, I'm not buying that shit, but I am going to talk to her because she will hear everything that Aunt Lisa will never tell her.

"Sariyah, no that is not a good idea."

"Auntie, you going to tell a pregnant woman no."

"You are pregnant?" Claudia asks looking down at my stomach

"Yes, I am."

"Lisa, please let me have one conversation with her."

"Marcellus ain't gonna be too happy about this shit."

"Who is going to tell him?"

We silently ride up to the apartment. This has to be the longest elevator ride I have ever experienced. I can see the concern in Aunt Lisa's eyes. She didn't know what to expect from me. I am really a sweet person until I am taken to a point I can't return from. She also knows I have a lot of animosity towards Claudia for many reasons and that this is definitely not going to be the way Claudia wants it to be.

"You said your name is Sariyah?" Claudia says as soon as we sit down at the table.

"Yes."

"That's a beautiful name for such a beautiful woman."

"Thank you, but let's be real, you don't want to talk to me, you want to know about your son."

"That's not true, I want to know you and him and hopefully be in my grandchild's life."

"Well, Marcellus is an amazing man, no thanks to you Claudia."

"Sariyah, calm down." Aunt Lisa knows it's time to intervene.

"Excuse me?" Claudia rolls her eyes.

"I'm madly in love with your son. On a daily basis, I deal with the pain you caused him, knowing his mother is a deadbeat. Thank god your sister took great care of him and loves him enough for the both of you."

"You don't even know what you are talking about!"

"Oh yes I do, I've been with Marcellus for 5 years and you don't even know my name. Let's not talk about all the other shit you missed. You didn't know he was the valedictorian when he graduated or played college basketball. Do you know he has an accountant degree and knows money better than anybody else?"

I have tears in my eyes for him as his mother looks at me like what I am saying isn't true. She is speechless. She gets up from the table and walks towards the door.

"You not ready for him to grace you with his presence because you still running away like you been doing all his life. You still have so much growing to do."

His mother looks at me and grabs the doorknob.

"Clearly, you will be a better mother than I ever was." Claudia walks out the door and doesn't look back.

"SARIYAH! Damn, I need a few shots after that shit." Aunt Lisa goes straight to her counter and pours her a shot of Patron.

"She deserves every word I said to her."

"You don't think you was a bit harsh."

"You need to stop defending her, you have been doing it for years and it's going to bite you in the ass soon."
I am getting a little carried away with my emotions, but Aunt Lisa knows she is too nice to Claudia.

"I know you are in your feelings or whatever, but girl you better watch yourself." Aunt Lisa says throwing back her second shot. "Now let's plan this party before I send your ass home."
For the next couple of hours, we plan the whole gender reveal party. I am overly excited about this baby and we will spoil him or her more than ever. The experiences I just had with Claudia and my mother made me realize being a mother is always a choice. You can take responsibility or walk away cowardly. For me, there is no question of what my decision will be.

I'm so excited to take this trip with Adonis. On top of being a nervous wreck, I'm still trying to get over the fact that I found happiness after such a down time in my life. I thought I could never love again and that all niggas were the same. Now, Adonis isn't perfect but, the way he treats me is just right.

I got out the shower when I hear a commotion in the kitchen. I immediately run to my bag and pull out my knife. I slip on some clothes and ready to stab the shit out of whoever is in my house. I have been so cautious lately. I tiptoe through the hallway and peel into the kitchen.

"Look who it is," I smile. "How the hell did you get in here?"

"I know you didn't think I renovated and didn't give myself a set of keys." Adonis picks up his keys and dangled them "Is that a problem?"

"No, but why didn't you tell me, I was about to stab your ass up."

"Honestly, it slipped my mind but why you didn't answer my 5 calls, I had to come to make sure you wasn't dodging my calls."

"My other nigga just jumped out the window, you can probably still catch him." I say laughing

"Sin, that's not fucking funny, don't play with me."

"I'm sorry, baby." I run over and give him a bunch of kisses.

"I'm serious, I know why that nigga was crazy about you. Imma say it once, if you ever think another nigga can have you, think again. I will do everything in my motherfucking power to keep you." Adonis makes eye contact with me and I can see the seriousness in his eyes.

"Same for you, you know I don't play that shit."

"So that we have agreed, let's get on the road." Adonis says, "We flying out of the airport in Connecticut."
Sariyah is going to kill me. I haven't even caught her up on all the things that have been going on because she is going through so much. I'll shoot her a text and hopefully she doesn't tear me apart.

Me: Riy, we had to take an emergency trip to see Adonis parents, we are heading to pick up his daughter now and then flying out tomorrow

Sariyah: daughter?

Fuck!

Me: yea, he has a 6-year-old in Connecticut. We haven't had a chance to catch up, but I love you and we will talk when I get back

Sariyah: No bitch, you going to call me right now.

Me: I can't, we are about to leave.

Sariyah: I will not let you stress me out but I'm going to kill you when I see you. Where do his parents live?

I don't even know where his parents live. What the hell am I doing? I usually ask a million questions and this time I just said "yeah" and dropped everything to be with him.

"Sin, go get your stuff so I can put it in the car."
I went to my room and got my luggage and my 2 totes.

"What the fuck? We going for a few days, not moving there."

"Where is there exactly?"

"Oh shit, you don't even know where are going." Adonis laughs "They live in Atlanta."

"I wouldn't mind moving there."

"Hell no, I need to be far away from my father."
The whole ride to Connecticut, Adonis tells me all there is to know about his parents and his daughter, Anais. But he isn't getting to the shit I'm really interested in and that is his history with Anais' mother. So, the only thing I can do is listen until he is done talking and ask him myself.

"You think you ready for this?"

"As ready as I am going to be."

"I booked a room at the Hilton but, we have to get up early to pick up Anais."

"Okay, no problem." Now is the time for me to get the real scoop. "Tell me about her mother and if I need to be prepared for some shade."

"I'm going to be honest with you, she doesn't know you are coming nor, does she know about you."

"Are you fucking kidding me?"

"Honestly, it's none of her business."

"Or you don't want her to know about me."

"Kaysin, you can't be serious."

Instantly I get upset and shut down. The feeling of disloyalty and dishonesty overcame me like no other. Instead of me spazzing out, I close my eyes until I can drift off into a comfortable sleep. Before I know it, we are pulling up to the Hilton and I want to go home.

"So, you not talking to me now." Adonis asks as he tries to lean in for a kiss.

I get out the car, grab my bags out the trunk and walk into the hotel lobby. I stand off to the side as Adonis gets the room keys and I follow behind him. Once we get to the hotel room, I get undressed and go straight to the bathroom.

"Yea, I just got in town, but I will pick her up in the morning." Adonis laughs. "Nah I'm staying at a hotel tonight, I'll see y'all in the morning."

"What the fuck is so funny?" I storm out the bathroom so fast.

"What are you tripping for?"

"See, you got me fucked up Adonis, you could've told her now, I was with you and you choose not to." I am heated. "You keep asking me if I'm ready, but your ass isn't ready."

"Sin, nothing is going to change, you are my girl and we going to get her in the morning than going to see my parents."

"Nah, I'm not going anywhere but home."

"Sin, I wish you would try to fucking leave." Adonis yells. "You are coming with me and that's the end of the argument."

As bad as I want to leave this fucking hotel, something isn't allowing me to besides the fact that Adonis drove us out here. I really want to know why he is hiding me from her. I already had to deal with all these other females down Adonis' back in the beginning and now I have to deal with his daughter's mother. Going to the gym to blow off steam was the best thing for me to do.

As soon as I get out the room, I call Sariyah.

"Hey girl."

"Why you sound like that?"

"Adonis didn't tell his baby mother about me and I am going to this woman's house in the morning."

"Did you ask him why?"

"He said it's none of her business."

"I mean, it isn't any of her business who he is dating but it is her business who is around her child so, you need to make shit clear to him."

"He will not get it until shit hits the fan with us."

"And I'm just wondering how you forgot to tell me he had a whole child."

"It slipped my mind, it isn't a big deal as long as he does right by her and myself."

"Kaysin, the stepmother." Sariyah laughs

"Don't play with me Sariyah, the real mother."

"Oh my god, I'm about to be someone's mother."

"Let me get this workout in and head back to the room."

I work out for about an hour. Deep down, I hope that Adonis is sleep by the time I get back. That hope slowly fades away when I open the door and he is staring at me.

"Where the fuck were you?"

"In my skin." I head straight to the bathroom to shower.

Adonis really wants to bring me out of character tonight and I am ready for it.

Adonis

Kaysin been tripping since I told her I didn't put Sky on about our relationship. Honestly, I feel like it's none of Sky's fucking business who I date, and I really don't think she gives a fuck. I know deep down she thinks I still have feelings for Sky and that's not the case. I gotta fix this shit before the morning.

"Oh, in your skin, you are real fucking funny."

"No nigga, you are funny, and you can get ready to sleep in that chair." Kaysin yells from the bathroom.

She got me fucked up, I'm sleeping in this bed right beside her. It seems like forever for her to get out the shower. She climbs in the bed and gives me her back.

"So, we not going to talk about this."

"What the fuck is there to talk about Adonis, you made your decision clear as day."

"Aight, so don't talk, just listen." I take a deep breath and just go in. "Sky ain't the friendliest person in the world and you aren't the most personable when you feel attacked. I know if I catch her off guard, she won't be able to make this shit hard."

"Adonis, I am a grown ass woman and can handle myself. Sky will see that, now I won't disrespect her, but I won't let her disrespect me. Understand me?" She turns around and gives me the death stare.

"Yea, baby girl. I understand."

It's going to be some shit tomorrow not even I can prepare myself for. I don't even remember falling asleep, next thing I know it's time to get up. It's 5 am and time to get ready to get Anais.

"Kaysin, we gotta get ready. Our flight leaves at 11 and we still gotta scoop Anais."
Kaysin jumps up so fast and gets ready.

"You still mad at me."

"To be determined, I'm getting ready, you lucky I'm still going through with this trip." Kaysin grabs her suitcase and went in the bathroom.
I was ready in 15 minutes and of course, Kaysin is still in that bathroom. That's exactly why I woke her up early because she takes forever to get ready. About 45 minutes later, Kaysin walks out the bathroom looking like a fucking model.

"Damn, baby girl." I can't help but stare.

"Adonis, let's go, I'm ready."

"You do know we are traveling." Kaysin has on crop top with leggings and her Gucci sneakers with an oversized sweater over it.

"This is travel gear now let's go."
The ride to Sky's house is silent. I can feel the tension in the car and I am ready to see my daughter's pretty face, she could brighten my day no matter what I am going through. When we pulled up to the house, Kaysin's eyes widen.

"Your daughter's mother lives here." Kaysin says as she sees the mini mansion I purchased for Sky almost 6 years ago. It was my first big purchase when I started getting money. Though her and I weren't always on good terms, if it had to do with my daughter, she will always be well taken care of.

"Yes, this house is about 6 years old, but she keeps it looking good."

"Almost 6 years old, so that means you bought this house." Kaysin says with so much attitude.

"Yea, I bought this house, Kaysin and my daughter lives here." I grab her hand. "Listen, you don't have nothing to worry about."
We both get out the car and I held her hand all the way to the door.

She is holding my hand so damn tight, cutting off the circulation.

"Chill, we are good."

When Sky comes to the door dressed in only a sports bra and booty shorts on, I already know shit was about to hit the fan, but I keep my cool like everything is fine.

"Hello Adonis." Sky says with a big smile on her face and reaches in to give me a hug. I let go of Kaysin's hand and give her a half hug. "Who is this pretty lady?"

"This is my girl, Kaysin."

"Hi Kaysin, nice to meet you." She extends her hand and Kaysin shakes it.

This isn't so bad.

"Nice to meet you, I've heard so much about you and Anais."

"Oh, that's funny, I haven't heard a thing about you." Sky laughs "Will you be joining Adonis and Anais on this trip?"

"Yea, I will be."

"Oh really, going to meet the parents, that's nice." Sky is being shady as fuck. "Well, I see you have been taking care of Adonis well, because no one meets the parents. I mean I did, but we were together for over 7 years."

"Chill, Sky, where is Anais?"

"Daddddddy!" Seeing Anais lit me up so much. She is the best thing that ever happened to me. She jumps into my arms.

"Hi, I'm Anais." She says looking at Kaysin up and down. "You are beautiful, I really like your hair."

"Thank you, princess." Kaysin smiles.

"Daddy, is this your girlfriend?" Anais smiles.

"Yes, baby, her name is Kaysin."

I could see Sky's eyes burning a hole in Kaysin's face, so it's time to make a dash to the airport.

"Alright, it's time to head to the airport."

"Not so fast playboy let me holla at you for a minute." Sky says after she hugs and kisses Anais goodbye. "Go sit in the car baby girl, daddy will be just a minute."

Kaysin walks towards the car. "Oh no sweetie, you stay too."

"Let me tell you something, I don't play about my child and I don't know what this slick shit Adonis tried to pull bringing you to my house unannounced, but I guess you mean something to him since you are here." Sky turns to me and looks me dead in the eyes. "Adonis, you really tried it, but I see shit doesn't change with you, always full of surprises."

"Sky, this isn't a game, you are unpredictable, and I wanted y'all to meet without the bullshit and drama. Kaysin and I been kicking it for a few months now and she has been good to me since day one. I never see my parents and they may never see her again, the time is right."

"Whatever you say, Adonis." Sky says "Ya'll have a safe flight, let me know when you land."

"Aight."

Kaysin and I walk away hand in hand, and I must say I am feeling good.

Sky

I thought I would never feel heartache again but seeing Adonis holding hands with another woman felt like the day he left me all over again. I loved him more than I loved myself for so many years. I tried so many times to get over him not wanting to be with me anymore, but I could never grasp it. I relive that day every time I see him.

"Sky, we need to talk." Adonis comes into the house after another late night of him working.

It bothers me so much that he works all the time and can't spend all of his free time with Anais and I. We have been fighting nonstop for the past two weeks and it is only getting worse.

"Yea, we do." I approach him ready to let him have it once again.

"I can't do this anymore." Adonis says as he sits down on our couch.

"What the fuck are you saying?" My heart drops instantly when I look in his eyes.

"I am not in love with you anymore, you are so used to this lifestyle of me providing you with any and everything you want but, you don't give a shit about me."

"Are you kidding me? I can't believe my ears. I gave up my whole life for you and Anais. Quit my job and been home taking care of our child."

"I never asked you to quit your job and be a housewife, you saw all this fucking money coming in and just decided you didn't need to be *independent anymore. You made choices without even talking to me about it. I could've been bought you a business or open some shit for you, but you never wanted that."*

The tears form in my eyes and I couldn't control my anger. I scream and beat on his chest.

"You can't leave us, what am I supposed to do? I don't have shit." I cry, terrified that I didn't know what tomorrow will bring.

"I ain't no fuck nigga, Sky. You and baby girl can live here for the rest of your life, the shit is paid off already, you just got to keep the maintenance up and you will be good. Your resume is good, you can get another job."

"ADONIS, YOU CAN'T DO THIS!"

"Keep your fucking voice down, Anais is sleeping." Adonis has his hands on his head and looks stressed. "This shit ain't easy, Sky."

"So, let's make it work, I'll change, I'll do whatever you need me to do." I can't stop crying, my entire world is crashing before my eyes.

"There is nothing to work out, my decision has been made for a few months now. I have been your enabler, you need to get your shit together for our daughter. She will not think someone will hand everything to her."

"And what about her? How fucked up of you to walk out on her!"

"I would never walk out on my fucking child, you really out of your mind, but this shit right here, she don't need to see. She will understand we are happier separate."

"So, when are you leaving since you don't want to be here anymore?"

"I bought a spot in New York by the shop. This fucking travel is crazy."

"So, you moving back to New York and you already bought a place." I can't believe this shit. "You really serious about leaving."

"Sky, you know I ain't no dumb ass nigga, Anais will be taken care of, I'll hit you with some bread every week until you get a job but for sure, your ass is getting a job."

"I am not a fucking child, Adonis."

"I know you not and believe me; I love you and Anais with all of my heart, but I already know where this shit is going. Maybe, we will get back together. Right now, we both need space."

"Whatever the fuck you say, you know what fuck you, I hope you are happy with breaking up this family."

"Don't start that shit, I am not arguing with you." Adonis turns around and walks into our guest bedroom and closes the door.

That was three years ago and every day until today, I had hope, he would come home. I just knew he was coming home until I met Kaysin. The way he looks at her and defended her was just validation he was really feeling that bitch. She is beautiful and polite, all the shit he likes. My hopes slowly vanished and quickly turned to anger.

"Adonis bought a bitch to my house." I called the only person who still knew I was madly in love with him.

"Are you serious?"

"Yes, and I think he might actually love her." I cried so much that my eyes were puffy and nose runny.

"So, what you want to do?"

"I don't know, but it won't be happily ever after for them, I refuse seeing any other woman with my man."

"Whatever you want to do, I'm down." She sighs into the phone. "I got some shit to tell you."

"What's up?"

"Trey is missing."

"What do you mean missing?" Adonis mentioned nothing about Trey missing, am I that irrelevant in his life now? That's Anais' godfather though, he should've told me. He probably told Kaysin. She probably knows all his secrets, or does she?
He been missing for a few weeks now. He never came home one night, and I don't talk to Adonis so can you ask him what's up when you speak to him again?

"Of course, boo, why didn't you tell me earlier?"

"I just didn't know what to do, he might not even be missing, he could've just left my ass. He started making a lot more money in the past few months and he wasn't tryna tell me where he was getting it from."

"As soon as I hear from him, I will let you know."

Sariyah

I feel like hell on earth, someone could have told me pregnancy was not fun. This baby makes me never want to get pregnant again. I want to stay in bed all day and sleep. I am not motivated to do a damn thing.

"Babe, don't you have a client meeting today?" Marcellus asks as he came out the bathroom looking like a snack.

"Yes, and I don't want to go. Your child is taking a lot out of me."

"My child, that sounds so good rolling off your tongue. Now come give me a kiss.".

Things have been so good between us. After I had that meeting with Claudia, I kept it a secret. He is going to be so pissed when he finds out. I know it will devastate him. I betrayed him by meeting her and once again, keeping a secret from him. So, for now, the best thing to do is keep it to myself.

"You always motivate me to get out the bed with some kisses." I jump into his arms.

"Girl, you getting heavy now, next time give me some warning." Marcellus laughs as he catches me. "Now, I have to go before you make me late for work."

"Aren't you the boss?"

"Nah, I have to set an example for the knuckleheads under me."

"I love you, by the time I get out the shower, you will be gone."

"I love you too, Princess."

When I hear the door slam, I am so relived because I was two seconds from telling him what happened. I need to talk to someone about it and Kaysin is having her own drama and probably on a plane right now, so I only can call one other person.

"Hey baby, how are you feeling?"

"Auntie, I am dying." I tear up as soon as she picks up the phone.

"What's wrong?"

"I want to tell Celly about me meeting his mother and I hate keeping this secret from him."

"Well, baby girl you need to tell him."

I can feel the tears falling from my eyes and I can't control them.

"Why am I going through all of this right now?" I cried. "I have so much on my plate."

"You want me to come over?"

"Please, I have a meeting in a few hours, but I can use the company."

Knock Knock

"Hold on, Auntie, someone is at the door." I quickly throw on some clothes.

When I open the door, I can't believe my eyes.

"What are you doing here?" Marcellus says as he comes off the elevator.

"I came to talk to Sariyah."

"Sariyah?" Marcellus looks so confused

I'm just speechless.

To Be Continued.

About The Author

Monique LaShone was born and raised in the Bronx. Growing up, she had trouble expressing her feelings verbally. She turned to poetry and writing journal entries as an escape. Eventually writing short stories and fiction became her favorite past time. She plans to turn her writing into more than just a hobby, teaching lessons of love and life in every book. Two of her many inspirations are her children and she aspires to be more than just a woman who writes.

Her long tern goal is to change the dynamic of urban fiction, mixing raw and uncut content with an informative awareness to different situations that our society experiences.